Praise for *To*

"With his pitch-perfect ear for dialogue, his knack for crisp pacing, and his unerring eye for what might be called the milieu of functional dissolution, Rob Pierce has revealed himself in story after story as a poet of the luckless, the bard of the misbegotten. In the hero of his latest and best, *Tommy Shakes*, he has found his Frankie Machine."

—David Corbett, award-winning author

"Tight as a drum, vicious as a pitbull. I don't remember the last time I read something that scratched the scuzzy itch of noir as well as *Tommy Shakes*. Just, maybe don't read it with a full stomach."

—Rob Hart, author of *The Warehouse*

"When you pick up *Tommy Shakes*, make sure you have nothing to do, because you're not going to want to put this one down. Rob Pierce at the tip-top of his game."

—Eryk Pruitt, author of *What We Reckon*

"When I was in rehab, I read the book Crime Novels: American Noir of the '50s. Willeford, Goodis, Thompson, Highsmith, and Himes. Had it all. Wretchedness, duplicity, alcoholism, and hopelessness. *Tommy Shakes* by Rob Pierce would've slotted in there perfectly. Nobody does grim and grave better."

—Joe Clifford, author of *Junkie Love* and the Jay Porter Thriller Series

"Rob Pierce writes the downtrodden like Rodin casts bronze, and *Tommy Shakes* is his masterpiece."

—Benjamin Whitmer, author of *Cry Father* and *Pike*

"If you like the kind of noir that makes you want to break out the hand sanitizer, Rob Pierce is the King—and the King does not disappoint with *Tommy Shakes*. Hard and mean and in your face like noir ought to be."

—Todd Robinson, author of *Rough Trade*

"Pure noir prose. Dark, disturbing, devastating. A journey through Pierce's Oakland is a hellish thrill-ride. Or a thrilling hell-ride."

—Tom Pitts, author of *101* and *American Static*

"Tommy can't get a break, but it's not like he's out to give himself one. This book is as relentless as it is bleak, yet oddly inspiring. You won't just root for an underdog, you'll root for collapse!"

—Nick Mamatas, author of *I am Providence*

Praise for the Books by Rob Pierce

"Rob Pierce is one of the more imaginative literary voices in our new emerging era of noir. A writer concerned with real people in our bizarrely unreal world who's deserving of the awards and accolades starting to come his way."

—James Grady, author of *Last Days of the Condor*

TOMMY
SHAKES

OTHER TITLES BY ROB PIERCE

Uncle Dust
Vern in the Heat
The Things I Love Will Kill Me Yet
With the Right Enemies

ROB PIERCE

TOMMY SHAKES

Copyright © 2019 by Rob Pierce

All rights reserved. No part of the book may be reproduced in any form or by any electronic or mechanical means, including information storage and retrieval systems, without permission in writing from the publisher, except by a reviewer who may quote brief passages in a review.

All Due Respect
An imprint of Down & Out Books
3959 Van Dyke Road, Suite 265
Lutz, FL 33558
DownAndOutBooks.com

The characters and events in this book are fictitious. Any similarity to real persons, living or dead, is coincidental and not intended by the author.

Cover design by JT Lindroos

ISBN: 1-64396-034-2
ISBN-13: 978-1-64396-034-0

*For those who've loved me and left,
and those who've loved me and stayed.*

CHAPTER ONE

Tommy Shakes used to have a junk problem, that's how he got his name. Still shakes sometimes, like it's part of him now. This time he shivers, his glass falls from his hand and he hits the floor. Across the bar Eddie keeps taking care of customers. On Tommy's side they leave him on the ground.

Guy on his left: "He's an asshole."

On his right: "Yep."

And Carla, the kids, everyone knows he's here. It's night, he's always here. Carla's had to pick him up enough.

Tonight maybe he ain't getting up. And who cares if he does? He's a drunk. If he ever goes home to that pistol he bought for Carla and uses it on himself the world's out an asshole. He'll be missed—even assholes have friends—but the people who miss him won't matter as much as the people who won't. The people who'd have loved him if he lived right—that's the fucking problem. He might as well be dead.

He knows it but sits up on the barroom floor anyway.

"You okay?" Eddie says. "You can't be doin' that in here."

Tommy looks up. "Not drunk. Maybe sick."

Says it like he's about to puke. He stands, shaky. Early evening but some of the crowd is like this by now. Of course, they've been here a while. He's only been here a few minutes.

He looks serious at Eddie, grabs his beer glass tight, sits on his stool. "Got somethin' for me?"

"After that?" Eddie shakes his head. "I worry about you, Tommy. You seen a doctor? Doin' anything besides drink?"

"Just the booze, Eddie. You my doctor. And I need work. Iron out shit at home with that."

"You never struck me as a money problems guy."

Someone down the bar needs a drink. Eddie walks away.

Tommy sits quiet a minute, drinks his beer, finishes it a couple minutes later and waves to Eddie.

Eddie comes back and Tommy taps the top of his glass. "It don't gotta be the world, Eddie. Any kinda thing."

Eddie picks up the glass, talks as he turns away. "I'll look, but I gotta see you straighter 'n this."

"I'll go home, rest up. You see me in a couple days, I'll be fine. I'm never like this."

Eddie shakes his head, sets Tommy's filled glass on the bar. "Seen you like this before."

"I'm not on *nothin'*. Must be sick, I don't know. Find me somethin', Eddie. I don't get somethin', Carla's gonna kill me."

"You don't look good, Tommy. I got no work for men fallin' down."

"Thanks, Eddie. Back in a couple days. You'll see." Tommy stands.

"You gotta understand—guys gonna hear about this. You're already on probation. Not the usual kind; the

2

kind where no one trusts you on a job. Anyone takes you on, they gonna test you first."

Tommy's behind his stool, on his way out. "I know."

"Sure," Eddie says, "but you don't know how they gonna test. The man starts the fight don't get to make the rules."

Thing he wouldn't tell Eddie, it wasn't just the money with Carla. How he made it pissed her off too.

"You got this way you gotta live," she said, "this guy you gotta be. Don't matter it don't work with me or Malik. You're this guy who lives wild, drinks too much, does anything for money. I know you quit junk, that's good, but you didn't quit the life. Didn't quit being that guy."

She said it like he could just change and be some other guy. A thing women never see as their fault—he was the guy she met, and now she wanted him to change. Like he's her fucking hairstyle.

Tommy sits alone on the couch, TV low so it won't wake Carla or Malik. Glass in his hand, fifth of bourbon on the table in front of him. It's night and they're asleep even though it ain't late. Except for them.

His gut churns, hurts. Been like that a lot lately. He still loves Carla and it feels like she still loves him. He can't give up, they just love different. She said he only wanted sex. She was beautiful, who wouldn't? Thing is she's pissed at him and they ain't fucked in a long time.

I'll get good work again, he thinks. Takes a drink. Bring the money home, make you proud. That's what he's always been good at, what worries him now. She works too, has to. He always makes money, but he always blows it. And she's the one talks to Malik; the boy barely looks at him. It feels like she stole their son from him.

"You only talk about you," she said. "You never ask about us."

He knows, can't change what's already done. Just trying to fix what comes. Don't like what's coming.

He feels Carla wake beside him. No reason for him to get up. "Got work comin'," he says, his eyes open enough to watch her rise. His hand goes toward her bare shoulder but she's already out of bed.

She stands over him, don't look his way. "Same kind of work?"

"It pays. It helps." Knows he shoulda never opened his mouth.

"A real dad," she says, steps away. "A real husband." She grabs clothes from the closet and steps toward the bathroom. She'll change in there, where he won't see. "Would really help."

She enters the bathroom, shuts the door behind her. She's gonna be a while, spends all her money on lotions. Calls them her ablutions, whatever the fuck that means. She looks great, so fine. But she's supposed to look great for him, not the world. Fuck the world.

He wishes he never woke up. Lies awake, eyes closed. Waits for her to leave the bathroom. To leave the house. Can't stand to think of her smooth brown back and those perfect little tits. Wants to be inside her and she don't care. He's been wrong too many times, lied too many times, somehow talked her out of leaving so far. By now it's just about Malik. She wants him to be a better dad, she's told him that enough. This is his last chance for that. He's blown his last chance at everything else.

She'll take Malik to school when she leaves. When they're gone he'll get up, cook a ton of bacon with a big omelet and toast and lots of coffee. He don't like to cook but that shit's easy, easy to clean up too, then she won't bitch about that. Some day she'll take Malik for good. His only hope is a job that pays enough money she stops complaining how he makes it.

He wants her here forever but if they ain't gonna fuck he wants her gone *now*. Not forever but now. So he can load up on fuel without looking at her, then go see Eddie and get work. Something where he can do good so he gets the big job next time. He needs the big job.

Seems like she'll never leave the fucking bathroom.

Eddie's a regular guy, works days at the bar so he can take real work when a night job comes. Mostly he sets stuff up, takes a piece of all that. But muscle work? He's a natural. Don't like the risk is all. Don't mind so much when the money's right. It's early and ain't many guys at the bar yet. He leans against it waiting for whoever comes. Like he's showing off the knuckles on his big hands, knuckles grown from all the times they broke. Hitting faces and anything else in the way.

Tommy pulls up a stool. "Hey, Eddie."

"Hey. The usual?"

"Just beer." Before Eddie pours a shot with it. "Lookin' for work. Hear anything?"

Eddie grabs a pint glass, turns his back to fill it. Sets it in front of Tommy, a five's already on the bar. Eddie looks at it.

"Whole lot more for you when you get somethin' for

me." Tommy drinks.

Eddie picks up the five, looks side to side. A bar lifer down either end, too far away to hear. Lowers his voice anyway. "I get five. You make at least two large, easy work. That's all I know about the job, all I wanna know. Serious work, Tommy." He drops to a whisper. "Fuck it up and I give him you, your wife, your kid on a fucking platter."

Tommy takes a short drink from his beer, looks up at Eddie. "Business always serious, Eddie. Why I ain't dead."

Eddie grabs a scrap of paper from under the register, sets it next to Tommy's beer, hands him a pencil. "Gimme your number. He calls you."

Tommy has a couple beers and leaves, his gut fucking killing him, like he might explode. Can't wait 'til he's healthy though, Carla could leave before then. Don't know when the job is, gotta be sober when his phone rings. It's in his pocket and it's charged. Two large ain't a ton of money but enough to be legit. And if he gets it soon, proves his worth, something bigger next.

He walks outside. Afternoon in the city, it's safe. This part of town anyway. Hears that ringtone that came with the phone, but he walks through crowds and it's always someone else's. Keeps walking. Life's good, work's gonna be good, he's gonna get Carla back, he fucking knows it. She loves him or she's already gone no matter what else is going on. That's how women work.

How he works? There's always someone needs a hand. If it sounds clean, he does it. Sounds messy, he says no. Agrees with Carla on that one—no time to serve time. He has a wife and kid to impress, and they can't hate or ignore or have pity on him.

Morning's gone and he's still walking. He was with Eddie less than an hour. It's three or four in the afternoon, breakfast has worn off. He steps into a pizza place.

"Pepperoni. Four slices." Two at this place would be a large meal for most. Tommy's always topped out at three. Sick as he's been, he should probably stop at two. "And a large Coke," he says when the slices arrive.

He takes a table for two, throws spicy peppers all over every slice. Don't know what that shit's called but it's good. Late for lunch and early for dinner, the place ain't crowded, no one sits near him. Good. Fuck people.

Almost done with the third slice, his phone rings.

"Yeah."

"We gon' meet before we work together."

"Yeah."

He gets a time, an address. He finishes his pizza.

"Tommy." Skinny guy he don't know sits at a back corner table outside, faces the street, the only way in. "Siddown."

Tommy never saw the guy before but he sits, faces him. "What's your name?"

"Not how this works. I tell you the deal. Take it, you know me. Don't, you don't."

Tommy stands. "I'm gettin' a beer. Need anything?"

Skinny taps the side of his coffee cup without looking at it. "I'm good."

I'm not, Tommy thinks as he steps inside. Not even tryin' to *get* good. More like a junkie, tryin' to get well. Maybe a beer settles his rumbling gut. And if things don't work out, get fucked up again.

Twenty feet inside the front door a fridge houses

shelves of bottled beers. Tommy grabs one. He could use a couple slugs before he talks to this guy. He reaches the counter, eight people ahead of him in line. He angles his beer bottle and pops the cap off the edge of the counter, drinks as the cap hits the floor. No one says shit. People in a place like this don't even wanna look at a guy like him.

The bottle's half empty when he reaches the register. "Just the beer," he says.

"Six bucks." Bearded guy at the register has an opener in his hand. Tommy takes a drink.

"How'd you get that open?"

Tommy pulls six bucks from his wallet and hands it to the guy, walks out the door. Something inside him wants to burst, gotta be nerves from Carla or maybe he's as sick as he feels. Like his gut could come out in any direction.

It's dusk, sun still up a little. The place has outside lights but they ain't on yet.

"Got a quick start on that," Skinny says.

"Here to do business, not fuck around." He sits. "What's the job?"

"No details here."

Tommy drinks. Guy talks like he's a fucking idiot. Won't be details at a place like this but the guy wanted to meet him, has to say enough for them both to decide.

"Just tell me what I gotta do. Ask me what you gotta know."

No one sits near them. Skinny looks around anyway, talks soft. "It's a bar, makes some book in back. Big day's the Super Bowl but they bring security for that. And Sundays the bar's packed, people watching games. But Saturday nights, regular season? Lotta money in back."

"In a safe."

Skinny shakes his head. "Not the whole time. They transfer it, don't do payoffs at the bar. Take the bets one place, pay off another."

"And you know when they pick up the money."

Skinny nods.

"And this ain't protected."

"All private, no one behind 'em."

"These guys nuts? Someone gets wind, they worse than dead."

"Why the job's safe." Skinny looks around again. Still no neighbors. "Just need a couple guys with guns to do this."

"How many guys they got? Including the driver. Cuz they *all* got guns. And no way I do this if they're Chinese or black. Those people cut a white man's balls off."

"Two guys pick up from one."

"So three. And there's a driver. Four. And you said a couple of us. We need more guys than they got and you provide weapons. I approve the weapons before I do the job."

"You ask the right questions," Skinny says. "But I gotta know about you."

"You know or you wouldn't ask." Tommy holds his empty bottle. "Be right back." He stands. "Need anything?"

"Nah."

Maybe Tommy's drink count matters tonight but fuck it, he ain't pretendin' he don't drink. Let 'em know this is who he is now. He stands in line, pays for his open beer when he gets to the register, goes back to the table.

Tommy sits.

Skinny's palm is over the top of his coffee cup. He tips his head up then back down, like maybe he's indicating Tommy's new beer. "And I'm supposed to believe you're fine."

"Beer and a shot now. Follow me the last two years, that's all you see."

Skinny holds his coffee cup again, like it's still warm enough to drink. "Whattaya do instead?"

"Instead of the highs?" Tommy shakes his head. "Work when it comes. Fight with the old lady. What's anyone do?"

"You shot heroin?" Skinny asks it casual, like it's a hobby.

"Everyone I knew did. Don't know none of them now."

"Ya want to?"

Tommy drinks, sets his bottle down. "Not guys you'd miss."

"What about the highs? Miss them?"

"The shit near killed me. Maybe that was okay then." He drinks. "Don't wanna die no more."

"So whydja fall down at the bar?"

Motherfucker Eddie. Business though. "Just sick. Don't last forever."

Skinny nods. "We leave here in separate cars. Prescott Motel, you know it?"

"Yeah."

"We meet in the parking lot, right outside where you check in."

No parking near the check-in building. Tommy pulls up in the red outside, waits. No one should want him dead right now, but if they do his foot's at the gas pedal and the engine's running. Probably Skinny just don't want

Tommy to know anything about him. There's gotta be someone else with him, and that's who's gonna pay for the room.

Tommy stays in his car, feels like he might puke. Sees a guy working behind the desk inside. If the guy looks, he can see Tommy too. See him or not, he don't come out.

A car pulls up behind Tommy. The driver gets out, walks up to Tommy's window, taps on it. Tall guy in a suit. Not too beefy but if he couldn't handle himself he wouldn't be here. Tommy keeps his window up.

"Wait here. We go to the room together." The tall guy goes into the building.

Tommy keeps his radio low, watches the building and the same skinny guy in the passenger seat of the car behind him, back and forth, one then the other, maybe five minutes.

The tall guy comes out, walks up to Tommy's window again. "Three-thirteen."

Tommy pulls around the lot. There's spaces, but no room numbers in the three hundreds. He keeps driving, around back of the main building. Parks in the next empty space he sees, checks the .38 in his shoulder holster—comes out easy if he needs it—and gets out of the car, walks to three-thirteen and waits outside.

The other car is right behind his, goes past where he waits and parks twenty feet away. The skinny guy and the tall guy get out and walk up to him.

Skinny talks.

"What're you packin'?"

Tommy's lips curl up.

"It's a job offer," Skinny says. "You won't get frisked. I want to make sure you come prepared. What're you packin'?"

"A .38 Ruger. Always."

"Nice." Then, to the tall guy in the suit: "Open the door."

The guy in the suit opens it.

Skinny walks in first. "Come on, Tommy."

"After your friend."

Skinny waves for the tall man to follow.

Tommy goes in third, shuts the door behind him. "We're here cuz you don't want an open door, right?"

"Lock it," Skinny says. The tall man walks behind Tommy and locks the door.

Tommy turns toward the man walking past him and something slams into the back of his head. Tommy staggers, falls to his knees.

"Got a gun at your head, Tommy. Where's your Ruger? My friend's gonna take it."

"Funny job offer." Tommy sounds drunk.

"Still what it is," Skinny says. "But we gotta check for track marks. Wouldn't want you wearin' a pistol and nothin' else."

"No fuckin' way I get naked."

The tall man swings again. The blow knocks Tommy's face into the motel carpet.

"Get that fucking pistol. And anything else he's carryin'."

Tommy's blinking fast as the tall guy squats over him, takes the pistol from his holster.

"Nice piece," Skinny says and takes it from the tall guy, who keeps searching. "When he can stand, he takes off his own damn clothes. Bad enough we gotta look at him."

Tommy's head throbs. Everything's blurry and he don't want to see anyway. He knows how it feels to be beaten, don't want to face whoever did this to him, not while they have the advantage. Jesus he feels sick. Holds back though. Don't like these guys but he needs the work. Might not get it if he throws up.

"Thought you could take a punch."

"Wasn't no punch," Tommy slurs. "I got hit."

No one talks, then there's a pair of shoes and the bottom of a pair of slacks in front of him but out of reach. The shoes are almost in focus.

"Gotta trust you if I'm gonna hire you," the voice says. "You know, first it's the junk, now you fall down in a bar. Fuck, you wanna work, Tommy? I gotta know you're clean. And you're on the fuckin' carpet. You can handle yourself in a fight, can'tcha?"

Tommy blinks. Skinny. A job. Money. Carla. "Gimme another shot at that motherfucker."

"Your next shot," Skinny says slow. "Take off your clothes, Tommy."

"What the fuck?"

"Checkin' for tracks. I don't trust an inch of you. Get up."

Taking off his clothes is an insult. Standing up is hard.

Tommy rolls onto his belly. Good, the only pain besides his gut is in his head. Nothing else new. But it hurts like hell and he don't know about his balance. Pushes himself to his feet. Lurches, stops the puke from coming.

They're both here, Skinny and the tall guy with the suit. The tall guy's pistol is at his side, pointed down. Too far away for Tommy to take it from him.

Tommy slips out of his jacket, lets it fall on the floor behind him, undoes his empty shoulder holster and drops it too. The shirt's buttoned and long-sleeved, must be what they're waiting for. He unbuttons down the front.

"This ain't a strip show, Tommy." Skinny holds Tommy's Ruger. Motherfucker.

"Goin' fast as I can. What he hit me with, a fuckin' pistol?"

No answer. Tommy finishes unbuttoning, undoes the first button at the bottom of each sleeve and throws the shirt down.

"Your fucking pants, Tommy," Skinny says.

Tommy looks at him but he ain't surprised. His head just ain't workin' right. "Gotta sit down, take off my shoes." Don't like the idea of any movement that affects the position of his gut. He waits until Skinny nods, then walks past him to the bed, sits with a grimace. He bends down, unties his shoes without falling, swallows deep to keep it all inside, and takes off his shoes and socks. He stands, unclips his pants and pushes them below his knees, steps out. He looks down at his boxers and takes them off too. "Gonna hose me down like I'm in prison again?"

Skinny grins and waves a hand and the tall guy in the suit steps toward Tommy, pistol in hand.

"We gonna look you over," Skinny says. "You got nothin' to hide, just hold still."

Holding still's more likely if Tommy knows the job's legit, but he don't know a fucking thing. The guy grabs Tommy's arm with one hand, aims his pistol at Tommy's gut with the other. Tommy watches his eyes, shuts his mouth tight.

The tall guy checks Tommy's arm for tracks, turns it at the elbow. Nothing. He looks at Tommy's other arm the same then pushes Tommy's head back, looks under his chin and on his neck.

Tommy swallows hard, exhales deep. "You gonna

shave my head so you can check there too?"

The tall guy moves his eyes down Tommy's chest, to his abdomen and below. "Damn right we're checkin' your head."

Tommy holds back as the tall guy checks too intently for marks on his dick and all around, across his thighs and to his feet. The pain in his gut's back at maximum strength. He shakes. The pain's everywhere.

"Turn around."

Tommy does. He feels like bending over. Maybe if he pukes…

The tall guy works his way up Tommy's legs to his ass, parts his cheeks. The guy stays there awhile, like Tommy might say something. The pain's all over and this motherfucker wants to stare into a shithole? Let him.

"You like it spread like this?" the tall guy whispers.

"Hey!" Skinny says.

And Tommy can't hold back anymore, spasms and shits all over the tall guy's head.

The guy pops up and slams his head farther into the shit coming down. Pulls away disgusted. Skinny screams "What the fuck?!" and Tommy turns and punches the shit-covered tall guy in the cheek, gets shit on his fist while what's coming out his ass trails him. The tall guy falls back and his head hits the carpet and Tommy kicks him in the ribs with the side of his foot, twice. The tall guy strains to breathe. Skinny aims the Ruger at Tommy and Tommy punches him in the temple with a shit-laden fist. Skinny and the Ruger fall in separate places.

Tommy drops to the floor hard and grabs his Ruger. Naked, shit on his fist and his ass and the backs of his legs, he stands slow. His body destroying him, he aims his Ruger at Skinny's head. "Now, what's this about a job?"

CHAPTER TWO

Get sick one time and he has to go through this bullshit audition. And now he's driving home a fucking mess. Cleaned up some in the bathroom but he had to keep an eye on those guys while he did. Just stood there in the shower, Ruger in hand away from the water, them close enough he could kill 'em, too far away for them to kill him. While he moved around and got clean as he could since the goddamn shower nozzle wouldn't adjust, wound up getting dressed with shit still on him. Hope Carla don't see him or his clothes like this.

Skinny's name is Smallwood. The tall guy in the suit's Dunbar. No way he's on either one's good side after the motel. He worries more about Dunbar. Don't know either one, but Smallwood's the planner, Dunbar the muscle. Planners cross you too, but show you can make them money and shit gets a lot less personal. Shit. Tommy laughs to himself as he drives, windows down so it don't stink so much. A little cold but it's November in California, he'll live.

Worries what he's doing to his car seat, pulls over first dumpster he sees, holds it open a few inches with one hand, paws around with the other. Can't see what gross stuff his hand grabs, don't want to neither. Hopes for some cardboard but that stuff's recycle money, might already be in the hands of a hundred-year-old Vietnamese woman. This ain't gonna work; even if he finds some newspaper in here it's gonna be coated in grease.

And he won't sit in his car again with nothing between his shit-smeared pants and the seat. He walks, not the best neighborhood but it ain't that late. Anyway, he figures he looks like an even worse choice than usual to fuck with. Probably a lump on his head and he don't care about that, never checked, busy winning the fight and turning himself into a shit monster.

Several blocks from where he left his car he finds a liquor store, walks in.

The white guy behind the counter looks disgusted. "Jesus mister, you can't come in here."

Must not be as bad a neighborhood as Tommy thought. He walks up to the register, opens his wallet, and puts two twenties on the counter. "A fifth a that." He points to a bottle of Knob Creek. "And where's the cardboard boxes you throw out?"

The guy's nose is crinkled but the twenties are in his hand. He rings up the bottle, bags it, gives Tommy a couple bucks' change. "Out back. Behind the store. Not inside."

The guy wants him to leave fast. Tommy has to stand still and smile. Ain't that easy to open a bottle of good bourbon or he'd start in the store.

He steps out front, pulls a knife from a pants pocket, cuts into the bottle's waxy seal and twists the lid off, takes a drink. Damn that's smooth. What a man needs on a night like this.

He closes the bottle, holds it by the neck so it's easy to swing if he needs to, walks around back and grabs two broken down boxes. Walks back to his car. No one better come at him now. Hate to waste a forty-dollar bottle on somebody's head.

Tommy pulls his black Impala into the one-car driveway. Carla's parked out front of the house. Whoever got home first parked on the street if they could, else the one who got home second might not park on the block. He gets out of the car slow, the shit on him drying, and drops the cardboard boxes on the ground. The drive home stunk even with the windows down but he ain't leaving them down while the car's parked. First thing after he cleans up he'll be back out here with air freshener.

He goes to the front door, keys in one hand, fifth of Knob Creek in the other. It's early, Carla and Malik will be up. No one should see him like this. Of course Rommel, the family pit bull, is just inside the door but he stands there, the quiet sentry, and lies down again. Tommy shuts the door soft, maybe he can make it down the short entry hall and to the bathroom unseen, walk out of there in a towel and smuggle his clothes into a fresh load of laundry.

Not quite. The hall opens into the kitchen and Carla's right there, Malik at the table with a bowl in front of him.

"Jesus," she says, "what's that?"

Like she's never seen a fifth in his hand. "You tell me. Ice cream in November?"

Her eyebrows rise. "You have to bring that in here?"

"Ooooh," from Malik.

"I'm sick." Tommy sets his fifth on the counter and hurtles out of there best he can, hopes nothing drops from his pants.

"Maybe it's your diet!" she yells and maybe it is, but he's sickened his whole family and that should be enough for now.

He breaks through the living room and toward the hall bathroom.

Carla follows with what must be long strides. He don't hear running but she don't lose ground. "You can't do this to Malik! He's our son, damn you!"

He can't have this conversation right now, turns his head enough to holler to her. "Gotta get to the bathroom!" He makes it and shuts the door behind him, drops his foul clothes.

She's right outside the door. "You think I wanna be in the same room with you?"

If he could see her he knows he'd want her, and with the shit on him reeking, he's about the ugliest man on the planet. But he turns on the shower knowing she always looks hot when she's mad. He knows because he's made her mad so many times. He steps into the water before it's hot enough in case she says something, turns his back to its stream so when the heat jumps it won't be aimed at his balls. Plus his ass is where the water's needed. Not that the rest of him is clean. He'll stay in here a while, maybe even after the water goes cold.

That smell has to go. And he has to get well so it don't come back, so Carla don't leave him. But right now he has to get himself together and work this job. Stop being sick and fucking up his marriage. And dammit their boy don't feel like his no more. She's the mom *and* the dad and he shoulda cut that off when he first saw it coming.

He's in the shower what feels like forever, the water cold for so long. He finally steps out. Drying is easy, ain't what he cares about. Now he's just cold. And the stink is still in the room. A towel wrapped around his waist, he opens the door, dirty clothes in hand, heads for the laundry room.

She's already there, leaning against the dryer, a glass of Knob Creek in her hand. She never drinks.

He nods. "Finish that glass, you'll be hurtin' in the morning."

She takes the tiniest sip. "I don't give a fuck about morning. Malik's old enough, he ignores me then anyway. You're the asshole worries me."

"At least I still count. Wasn't sure about that."

"You're his father," she says. "Act like it or not."

"I love Malik."

"Really? What does he do all day? What do you know?"

"I don't get him," he says. "Don't tell me I don't love him."

"You don't talk to him."

He walks past her.

"What the fuck are you doing?"

"Gotta clean my car. And you're drunk."

"Don't tell me about drunk."

"Know more about it than you." He keeps going, to the cabinet where they keep the air freshener. From there to the bedroom for a change of clothes, then to the car. Problem is, from the car it's back to the house and that ain't practical no more. Already knows he's gonna lie untouched on the bed. But where else is he gonna lie? Play this wrong, he'll have a lot of time to find out.

He sets the air freshener on the bedroom dresser, goes to the closet and drops his towel in the hamper. Stands there with his legs spread, not that he expects Carla to rush in wanting him but his body's been filthy and the air on his bare skin feels good. After a minute he pulls on a pair of pants, puts on a t-shirt and socks and walks outside to air out his car. God knows what it takes to get that smell out permanent. He over-sprays the front seat, the awful flowery scent better than the stink of shit, and returns to the kitchen.

Where his bourbon sits alone, his family no longer there. About a finger is missing from the bottle. Carla's drinking spree. He grabs a glass from the cabinet overhead and fills it, drinks. Maybe she's right, this is part of why he's sick, but it's also why he ain't completely insane. Killing the pain of what she does to him, and what she won't let him do to her.

He takes the bottle and glass to the kitchen table, sits and drinks. Has this job with Smallwood to think about. He's calmer by the time he finishes the glass. No thanks to Carla. She excites him, good or bad.

The living room's quiet, he goes out there. Dark and empty. Perfect. He sits on the couch, sets bottle and glass on the coffee table and fills up again. Looks like the whole house behind him has gone to bed. He turns on the TV, volume low, watches sports highlights and wonders where's this bar he's gonna rip off. And will he have to do something about Dunbar?

He keeps drinking and one of tonight's problems solves itself. He ain't getting off the goddamn couch. Except to grab a leather jacket from the hall closet, something besides the booze to keep him warm. Staggers back to the couch and works his way around it, plops himself down and into Rommel's bulk. Rommel barks and Tommy's off the couch. He sits there again and tries to work himself into a lying position but Rommel don't move. Tommy lies on his side like that will make him fit

21

but there's no space on the couch for his legs.

Fuck it, he eases himself to the carpeted floor, pulls his jacket down with him. He loves that dog.

He's shaken awake. Carla whispers, "Get into bed."

It's dark. He gets up, surprised she wants him in there. "Why?"

She's got him by the hand, don't answer as she leads him out of there and down the hall, into the bedroom. She shuts the door behind them and he tumbles into bed. She whispers again. "Malik shouldn't have to see you like that."

"I was just sleeping on the couch."

"You were on the floor."

She remains standing. He lies down, blinks at the bedside clock. Six a.m. This must be when she gets up and makes sure Malik gets ready. He guesses that, is never up this early himself. "My dad slept on the couch."

"The couch would be bad enough."

Weird how much anger is in those quiet words. It's true about Dad. Tommy grew up thinking that was where dads slept. Sometimes both his parents came out of the bedroom in the morning and he wondered what was going on. Of course Dad wound up leaving, but he was okay. Never home much and drank when he was there, but mostly stayed by himself in the house, worked the rest of the time. Worked a lot, sometimes all night.

Tommy knew better than that last part now, better understood why his parents yelled when they did talk. Still seemed like the normal way for a husband and wife to talk.

"Look," he says to Carla's back. She removes little

items from drawers and sets them on top of the dresser. "I'm tryin' to straighten out some work stuff and my health, get everything together and work things out with you."

She talks as she walks to the closet and opens it. "Look at the order you put those things in. You wanna work things out with someone, might wanna put them first."

She's got a dark red skirt out, turns in his direction as she holds it in front of her. When she puts it on it'll stop just above her knees, show off her lower legs and hint at her thighs. He's dying here, but she's turned toward him only out of habit. She sure as hell don't want anything to do with him right now.

She drapes the skirt over one arm and shuts the closet door, returns to the dresser only long enough to swoop the little things off it and step into the bathroom, shut the door behind her. In a minute the shower will be running. She's part of his hangover now, they're both killing him. He lies on his back, arm over his eyes, and hopes he can get back to sleep.

In another café with Smallwood, Tommy's choice this time, and he's drinking coffee late morning although he's sure he'll get to hair of the dog soon enough. Neither man looks good the morning after. Each took shots to the head.

"Gotta see this place," Tommy says. "Gotta see who runs it."

"Can't let them see you, though."

"Only way they see me is if you or your boy rat me out."

Smallwood shakes his head. "Don't mean to piss you off. Just some guys need to hear the obvious so I say it to everyone. I know you ain't one of 'em.'"

There's people at the next table. Tommy stands. "Let's take these to go." He walks with his coffee.

"Your cup." Smallwood stands without his, nods at the mug Tommy's leaving with.

Tommy keeps walking. Smallwood follows but now Tommy don't trust him, the guy ain't hard enough. They get on the sidewalk, out of anyone else's hearing range. "There's as much money as you say," he talks soft, "we might have to kill someone to take it. Who else is on this job?"

"You, me, and Dunbar so far."

"I pick the other guys or I'm out."

"That's not acceptable."

Tommy stops on the sidewalk so Smallwood has to stop with him or leave him behind. Smallwood stops.

"I'm lookin' at you, Smallwood, and I don't see a killer. Dunbar maybe, so maybe you can see it in guys, but I don't know how. I can see it, Smallwood. I've lived it, grown up with it. My life is fucked and if somebody gotta die to fix it…" Tommy shrugs. "I pick the guys."

Smallwood nods.

"And I don't know what the fuck you do." He resumes walking.

Smallwood joins him, angles his head, looks at Tommy. "You sayin I'm out?"

"It's your job, you still get your share. A big finder's fee."

"But I planned how it's done. I planned it with me part of it."

"Guess I gotta hear your plan then."

There's people near them now, more on the sidewalk ahead. Smallwood nods. "Okay, but not here."

They get in his car and they're off. The café was in a pleasant business district, overpriced restaurants and shops, even a bookstore. Tommy drives through that, into the suburbs beyond.

Smallwood don't argue, just sits there like he knows he's getting fucked. Not a thing a real gangster would do. Both men should wonder how this goes when it's time to split the money. But you gotta wonder that the whole time until a job's over, and until you worked with a guy a few times, you gotta wonder every time.

Tommy don't wonder, knows there's gonna be a double-cross, has to make sure he pulls his first.

Traffic thins and almost no one's on sidewalks, the occasional dog walker and that's it. Malik better get Rommel out today. He don't get his daily workout, he demands it at night. A big black-and-white thing, he'll run up and down the house barking and nipping at the air. Someone takes him out or he might do that all night.

"I need to know about the bar. I need to know your plan to rip it off. If the plan ain't good enough, I need to know so I can change it. So. What's the place?"

"It's called The Manatee. Know it?"

Tommy keeps driving and the small number of pedestrians fades to none. The houses are still nice until that's just some of the houses. The other houses look like they used to be nice.

"Near the lake, right?"

Smallwood nods.

"Been past, ain't been in. Looks too decent for gambling or maybe I would."

"That's the cover," Smallwood says. "It ain't like one

25

of these Chinatown places in the city, with point spreads running across a LED over the bar. Not a black joint either, that was your other worry. White guys run a respectable place in front. Gambling's in back, different crowd there. I mean, gamblers are anyone, security might be anyone, but guys in charge are white. Not mobbed up, either."

"Just waiting to die and don't know it."

"Exactly," Smallwood says.

There's suburbs and there's Oakland suburbs—too many of the old houses run down, sagging, remnants of what they were, like a beautiful woman who had too many face lifts. What crime does to a man when it don't pay, it can also do to a house. So you drive past one house and it's well maintained, the next not so much, then something's been converted into a triplex and something else torn down altogether and replaced by ugly apartments. Some houses in the process of being torn down or remodeled. The change happens one block to the next.

"Sounds safe to go in the front then. They serve dinner, right?"

"I ain't eating there."

"Don't mean you. Me and one of my guys." Tommy grabs his gut. "Ah Jesus."

Tommy and Smallwood are out of the regular suburbs, into the Oakland suburbs, and soon they'll be out of neighborhoods and into a stretch off the freeway where nice businesses failed. Replaced by liquor stores, nasty takeout places, and ugly motels. And on further to somewhere seedier. Where everything's cheap and what's illegal's cheaper. Every building looks like it could crumble any minute and there's no way the landlord repairs it because no one down here has any money. These are apartments lived in by men and women who look already dead; the only evidence they're alive is how loudly they're insane.

Tommy pulls off the road, opens his door. He bends over, turns to his right and pukes violently, his head lurching hard forward and back. The vomit's a pile on the side of the road. Smallwood covers his nose with one arm.

Tommy closes the car door, coughs, exhales mouth wide, feels the brutality of his breath. "I need the layout of the place and your plan in writing. Then me and my guy check it out."

"Can we get outta here now?"

"Yeah, this neighborhood makes me sick."

CHAPTER THREE

Juke ain't one of these know-it-all young fucks, he knows what he's doing and he keeps his mouth shut about it. He stands at the bar in his black leather jacket and faces the door. T-shirt and jeans, his haircut close and crisp, looks like a male model only Juke's no faggot. Tommy walks in and Juke raises his beer bottle, waits until Tommy has his drink and they're both seated.

"So, work?"

"Hope so. We gotta go to dinner, check the place out. Finish these," Tommy raises his beer, "I explain on the way over. We decide to do the job, I gotta bring in at least one more guy."

"Who?"

"I see the job, I have a better idea. Right now I'm thinking muscle."

Juke nods. He knows guys but don't say a word. Tommy knows guys too. If it's just muscle, everybody knows guys.

They finish their beers and Tommy drives. "This other guy—I won't say his name 'til I know you're in—has a plan, real basic. See, it's a restaurant with a bar, and in back they take bets but they pay off somewhere else. So every Saturday night they pick up the money, take it wherever they pay off. His plan is, while everyone's inside, one guy takes out the driver, then when they come out, we got 'em outnumbered and we take the money. I wanna see the place tonight. The way I'm thinkin', it's smoother if we rip it off Friday night when their delivery guys ain't there. A little less money but a lot better odds."

"But you're still lookin' at the extra money if we pull the job Saturday."

The kid's smart, part of why Tommy likes him. "Yeah. This looks okay tonight, I'll be outside Saturday. But I also gotta know what it looks like inside."

The Manatee might be a nice place, but not so nice it has its own parking lot. It's on the east side of the lake, one of the only businesses down that way, but there's no parking around there at dinner time. "We might cancel this job cuz of parking," he says, waiting to turn left on a residential street.

"Fuckin' lake," Juke nods. "Everybody loves the fuckin' lake."

Something they actually cleaned up in Oakland and it might fuck with this job. Tommy shakes his head. Goddamn city only fixes things that already work.

Anyway, people think the lake's romantic, safe, go out walking on dates at night or jogging late, with their jewelry and their smartphones. Every few years there's a mugging spree for a couple months. That'd be the fuckedest thing. Pull the job then get ripped off at gunpoint taking it to the car.

There's a space and Tommy pulls in. "Parking gotta be better late night. I'll find out before I decide."

Juke don't even nod at that, just gets out of the car. Walking to the place is all that's needed now. They get there, ask for a table for two, wait at the bar. Juke's good-looking but one glance at Tommy and no way it looks like a date. Tommy wishes Juke was uglier anyway.

They talk about nothing that matters and have beers at the bar, look around.

It's a regular restaurant, nothing fancy but every table full, the long bar crowded. There's a lot of good food in Oakland but nothing along this stretch, so it's a great location. Still, there's a ton of places on the other side of the lake and it has to compete with those.

"Don't know what's on the menu," Tommy says, "but I bet we eat good."

"Food ain't why I'm here."

"Place is crowded," Tommy says. "I wanna know why everyone else is here."

Juke nods.

Tommy drinks, surveys the room. Friday night and the tables are filled with nicely dressed couples in their thirties and up. The guy at the door said the wait was fifteen minutes to half an hour, so it ain't that packed and this is seven p.m. Still, it's doing well. Not the rich crowd or the younger crowd, more like middle-class, middle-aged. Add to that in either direction and you're doing fine on legit money alone. Plus the gambling take.

Make enough money in a place like this you could fill a couple tables with protection. Guys who eat here every night. Guys who never leave. Guys who shoot you in the back when you think you got everyone outnumbered. Juke's good, but he ain't been through all the shit Tommy has.

"Ask where's the toilet."

Juke waits until the bartender's near them, asks question and heads off in the direction the bartender sends him. He follows a narrow carpet fifty feet past all the dinner tables. At a wall where the sign says Restrooms and points left, he looks around for a bit before turning left. Tommy has a table by the time he returns, stands so Juke sees him. Juke sits and gives Tommy the route to the back room.

Tommy nods. That has to be where the gambling happens.

Tommy looks around for a waiter, waves like he's drowning. A man in something resembling a tux shirt and vest shows up.

"I need a drink," Tommy says. "Knob Creek if you got it."

"Yes, sir." The waiter tips his head and walks away.

Tommy sips water. Good thing he can hold his liquor. Mainly he hopes he don't get sick again. No shitting or puking until he's home tonight.

Tommy's drink is set in front of him. "How long on the food?" he says to the waiter.

"I'm sure it will be soon, sir. But I only serve drinks." He walks away.

Tommy looks hard at Juke. "Fucking servants. Always know what the other guy does. Or he might do it to you."

"That's our line of work, not his."

"Still…"

"You hungry?" Juke says.

"Just don't like chickenshit answers. And yeah, I could use some food."

"We ain't been here long."

"You on their side now? Who the fuck wants to pull a job with ya?"

"Fuck off, Tommy. Food might be a while is all."

"Yeah," Tommy says. "Don't make me less hungry. And I can't go to the back too soon. Gotta have a couple drinks first."

"So have 'em."

Knob Creek's good stuff, definitely sipping whiskey. Tommy takes a sip. A long sip. Again. One more and it's gone and he's waving for a waiter. Keep those drinks comin'.

After a while the meal arrives. They eat and Tommy has a couple more rounds and it gets to be time. Tommy pushes his chair back, stands a little shaky. Juke points toward the men's room and Tommy starts that way, almost gets there, and takes the carpet where it leads in the other direction.

A big ugly man guards the door at the end. No way anyone gets in by accident.

Tommy steps to the door.

"You here for somethin'?" the ugly guy says.

"A football game," Tommy says. "There's money at stake."

The ugly man opens the door and Tommy walks into what looks like a sportsbook at low tide. There's a barred window and whoever works it must be farther back. No other customers, no one Tommy can see.

The room's maybe thirty feet deep before you hit the window. Ten feet before that is a row of chairs you might find at a card table, like a game's about to break out. So everything Tommy's gonna care about is the other side of the barrier.

He walks up to the window and no one's there. He talks loud. "I want the Niners and the points. Line's thirteen. You giving thirteen? I got a yard on this." The Niners were terrible, but not so bad against the spread. They kept most games close.

Tommy looks in but it's like a goddamn bank—nothing of interest where you can see it. There's a guy wearing glasses in the room behind the windows. More important, there's a door beyond that room, and somewhere back there is where the real money is.

The guy in the glasses shows up at the window. Vest, pinstriped shirt, like an actor playing the guy who works at the illegal book. "Yeah," he says quiet, like it matters, "the line's thirteen."

Tommy opens his wallet and counts out twenties.

"Put it in the slot," the guy with glasses says, "you get a ticket." The slot is a sloped metal tray that levels out under the gap in the glass, basically the same setup as a cheap hotel but with thicker glass.

Tommy slides the money forward, gets a ticket back like for a ride at the county fair. Looks down the counter. Far end there's a door for employees to get behind the counter, a buzzer on the wall beside it, just like a fucking bank. A doorway straight to the money. Fucking minor league.

"You learned something back there, right?" Juke looks eager.

"Yeah." Tommy shakes his head. His leg is cramping but he's standing, it'll stop. His arms shake. He presses them to his sides so no one notices. "If we do it Saturday, gotta do the job outside. Too easy for someone to get behind ya inside."

"And Friday?"

"Right guys, it can be done."

"Gotta see the exchange first for outside though, right?"

"A few times. Make sure they don't change things up. And talk to my guy with the plan. See how he thinks we should do this and what else he knows."

"We done here for the night?" Juke has both hands on the table like he's about to stand up.

Tommy sits. "Another round. Then we go."

They finish this round and order the next. Tommy starts on his new glass and bolts up, slams the near full glass back on the table and runs to the bathroom. Starts to anyway, but there's people in the way and he has to slow down to get around them. And he's shaking. He grimaces and grunts and walks fast as he can. Some people hear him and get out of the way. "Excuse me, excuse me," he mumbles, weak like the crowd now, not wanting to open his mouth in case he pukes instead of shits. Glad whatever sick's in him has stayed inside so far.

Somehow he makes it to the stall, gets his pants off and sits without shutting the door. The shit bursts from him, his head toward the floor and eyes squeezed shut, teeth clenched. He feels emptied out, sits there a couple more minutes to make sure, rises slow and shuts the stall door. He shakes like crazy and sits again. When the shaking stops he starts wiping his ass, glad at least they got decent toilet paper here, not that fucking one ply. And he thinks maybe he's getting better, he made it to the toilet this time. Jesus, he may be better but he sure ain't well. Hopes they got enough toilet paper, feels like a world's worth of shit is stuck on his ass.

A few more minutes and he's done, stands and flushes. It's one of those power toilets, roars and swallows all that paper and shit, all but what's stuck on the sides. Tommy stands there, not that he wants to stay, but he don't feel like moving either. Stays until the toilet's done flushing, flushes again. He's just that nice a guy.

He walks out of the bathroom head down, back to the table where Juke has just started his next beer. A full one for Tommy sits there but he opens his wallet, hands all the cash to Juke. It's his restaurant budget; no way he uses a credit card for something like this. "Meet me at the car."

He walks steady as he can to the door, looking down. Last thing he wants is to be noticed tonight. Fuck being sick, might blow this job for him. And he needs this job.

In a couple minutes Juke opens the passenger door, gets in. "Man, I don't know."

Tommy pulls away from the curb. "Don't know what?"

"*Anyone* pulls a job here someone might remember you. They'll be lookin' at guys who mighta did it, and anyone sees your face might remember tonight. Fuck, how many times a big guy like you run through here? I don't know, man."

"Always reasons not to do a thing. Reasons to do it weigh more."

Juke turns sideways to look at him but Tommy watches traffic. "Yeah, well," Juke says, "my reason to do this is money. Straight up. Don't got an old lady gonna leave me if I don't—"

"Shut up."

"Nah, Tommy, I'm talkin' true here. I like you, man, but I'm not *like* you. My life don't suck. With this job, you fix shit. I just buy shit."

Tommy swings the wheel hard right, pulls to the curb

fast, rolls down his window, sticks his head out and throws up in the street. The car driving past barely misses getting hit and Tommy sees the driver's finger aimed at him. Just a finger, no reason to duck, and he pukes again, gets another finger from the next driver. Now he's looking to pull back into traffic, feels weak and his head throbs.

No opening yet, he looks at Juke instead of traffic. "You old enough to know Tino One Hand?"

Juke laughs. "That a real name?"

"His dad wasn't Mister One Hand but yeah, Tino One Hand's a real name. Lotta years ago, Tino's young then, there's a war going on around here. Some fuck with a axe chops off Tino's right arm halfway down from the elbow, but the guy gets shot by Tino's partner and dies, leaves Tino alive. The partner wraps up Tino good enough he don't bleed out, gets him to a guy who stitches him up.

"So now he got just one hand, and it's his bad hand. I mean, he was right handed, nothing wrong with the left. But he's a guy with one hand and it's weak and he's young but he don't know no other life, don't want to. So he turns that hand into a good hand, I mean like they say blind guys hear better, shit like that?"

Juke nods. "Yeah, heard that."

"This motherfucker Tino goes crazy working that left hand, more strength there than most guys got in two. And he's muscle, he gotta go to his boss and prove he can do his old job. Shows up at some guy's door to shake him down for what he owes, guy laughs at the fuckin' cripple and Tino has him in the air by the neck. Don't just lift the guy either, he's fuckin' strangling the motherfucker. Holds him 'til the guy passes out, drops

36

him, takes everything the guy has, and word gets out. Do *not* fuck with Tino One Hand.

"So there's the world, not fuckin' with him, but that kinda work makes enemies. Sometimes some asshole comes at ya. Tino drops those guys too, and he don't always leave 'em breathin'."

"Guys don't know how to do a hit?"

"Always just some pissed off asshole. No *boss* is after Tino, this is business on his own turf. Guys just do stupid shit."

"What's this gotta do with me?"

"Just sayin'," Tommy says, "there's reasons to quit. Tino had reasons to quit the whole life."

"So how old's this guy?"

Tommy shrugs. "Not wanting to quit ain't enough. Ya always gotta be ready, ya gotta have good habits. Tino had all that, almost all good habits. One bad one, though. Ever see a guy sittin' on a barstool, hooks his feet under it?"

Juke nods. "Yeah, sure."

"Tino did that. He also drank. Not a bad habit if you can handle it, and he could. Tino sits in the bar like always one night, don't know if he catches tail there sometimes or he just likes the bar, but someone else knows he likes the place and that someone don't like Tino. Some crazy ex-Marine, Tino fucked up his little brother, clean job, what he's paid to do, but the jarhead don't care about that. He knows what Tino looks like, goes up to him at the bar and sucker punches him. Tino falls back, takes the stool with him. Probably broke an ankle. Not sure. Tino tries to get up, falls back down, and the guy shoots him in the face."

"Jesus."

"Yeah. Guys who ain't in the life are more trouble than they're fuckin' worth."

"Still—what the fuck's this got to do with me?"

Tommy tilts his head back, looks up and sighs. "Don't gotta quit just cuz it looks like you should. Also don't go into shit with *any* weaknesses. This job's gonna happen and I'm gonna run it. You're in if you want. Only I can't do it right away. Might have to run and take a shit before we got the money."

Juke laughs.

"I'll tell Smallwood his plan's suicide. Then I tell him I got one that works but needs time to set up. When I feel good, we pull the job. You in?"

"We meet when you feel good," Juke says. "Then I decide."

Tommy nods, checks traffic again, pulls into the street when it's clear, shakes his head. "Me and Tino One Hand. We got no other life. Gotta pull jobs 'til there's no jobs left to pull. And there's always jobs."

Juke don't answer. The car's quiet a minute.

"Whatta they call that," Tommy says, "job security?"

Sounds like a joke. Juke laughs.

"Not kiddin' here," Tommy says. "Always some asshole got money just askin' to be took. Sometimes I'm the guy gets to take it. There's always enough assholes."

Juke nods. They ride quiet all the way to his place. "Get well," he says, getting out of the car. "Then we work together."

Tommy nods, don't say shit. Gets to his place, Carla's parked in the driveway but there's a spot on the street right out front. He takes it, goes inside, his gut ripping him up, turns on the TV and lies on the couch, Rommel not here for a change. Basketball, good enough, he don't

38

care what teams. Just some action he can watch with the volume down, and he won't drink no more tonight. Maybe she's right about that. He don't hear her or Malik but they're home and it's too early for everyone to be asleep. Not too early to have headsets on at their laptops though. Fine, he'd be lousy company right now. Talk to everyone tomorrow, he'll be a day closer to healthy or dead. Either way a good thing. But he better not die like this, with Carla not just pissed but disgusted, thinking he's some fat drunk crook. He ain't that fat.

He knows the other shit means more, but of course he's a crook, he's good at it, and yeah he likes to drink, he's good at that too. It's weird he gets along real fast with strangers, figures they're a bunch of suckers easily played, any nice thing he says counts as charming. Bullshit he was taught as a kid, how to make it through school even though he was always in trouble. Living with someone's harder, connecting on stuff they call real. Only real he knows is staying alive, sometimes when other people want you dead. Right now marriage feels harder than that.

Fuck it, this ballgame's gonna end and he'll be here on the couch alone but he won't have to stay. Just too early to sleep and one thing he don't feel right now is horny. Good, because Carla's gonna push him away anyway. Like all he cares about is sex, when it's sex with *her* that makes him crazy. She don't get how much he loves her and how this is the only way he can show it, words don't work and no matter what she says, he don't believe they ever did.

He sits alone on the couch in the quiet house and watches the end of the game. Someone wins and someone loses and he don't care who. He watches highlights after that, all the games, and football previews and injury reports, nothing that has a damn thing to do with his life. It all flies by, a waste of time. Entertainment. He's good with how it passes the time but that's all it does. It gets late and after a couple trips to the toilet his stomach settles some and he heads off to the bedroom.

He stands just inside the door until his eyes adjust to the dark. Carla lies in bed, eyes closed. He crosses the room, takes his clothes off at the bed and drops them to the floor, puts on a pair of sweats and gets into bed beside her.

Her eyes flip open. "Get out." The words soft, her mouth barely open.

"What?" He stays where he is, tired now, his answer a grumble.

"Get out. You snore."

"Can't do nothin' 'bout that."

"Told you this before." She sits up. "Booze makes you snore. You still drink. Stop and maybe you can sleep here."

She lies back down, turns on her side away from him.

"Fuck." He gets out of bed. He could argue but they'd wake Malik. He steps over his pants and shirt to the closet, opens it and grabs a spare blanket, leaves the closet door open and walks the fuck out of the bedroom, shuts the door quiet but he's pissed as he goes back to the couch, lies down with his legs pulled up so he don't kick Rommel. She's the one don't want him sleeping here, guess that don't matter now. God knows what set her off tonight but now's the wrong time to argue.

He was ready to sleep beside her but now he's alone and on the couch five minutes and he knows he ain't about to sleep. And it's not because of Rommel. He won't get comfortable because of the dog but he's a married man, he can sleep uncomfortable. He turns the TV on like there's another sports update since the last one, walks into the kitchen and grabs what's left of his fifth of bourbon and a tall drinking glass, returns to the couch and pours the glass full.

He drinks, picks up the remote and surfs channels until he hits a movie he's seen before, something he can watch even if he can't hear it. He drinks knowing he don't want to, maybe this is why he's sick but he can start getting well tomorrow, talk to Carla tomorrow. The movie's a crime flick and one of the actors looks like maybe he's hard but the rest look like actors and Tommy knows he hated this piece of shit movie when he saw it before, maybe with Carla or why else. He hates the way it looks, don't listen to what it says, drinks and drinks more. She probably kicks him off the couch at six a.m. so Malik don't see him but then he gets to drop onto the bed when she's off it. Worst time but at least he can go back to sleep. She never gave him a chance to say he's taking time off work to get well, that he won't be drinking. She might get glad and hopeful if she believes him and he'll have to say it ain't like that, he's just quitting the booze 'til he ain't sick. But it won't come to that, she won't believe him.

He looks at the stupid fucking movie. Might as well finish this bottle tonight, he ain't drinking tomorrow.

CHAPTER FOUR

She shakes his shoulder, the room dark and his head raging.

"Throw that away." She points at the empty Knob Creek bottle. "Get into bed. Now. I'm getting Malik up."

He sways awkwardly into the kitchen fully dressed and drops the bottle in the wastebasket, makes it to the half-bath down the hall, sits on the toilet but only pisses. He gives up on shitting and stands, expects to turn and vomit violently, but the barrage sticks behind the back of his throat. Nothing but poison inside him and none of it's coming out.

He works his way slow down the hall, certain he looks as bad as he feels. Malik's too young to see his dad look like this. Tommy makes it to the bed and shudders, crawls in, and pulls the blankets over his head. Total darkness and a lack of oxygen, maybe that'll be enough to let him sleep. He lies on his back like Carla always tells him not to, it'll make him snore. But if booze causes snoring he's bound to anyway.

He needs to get some sleep then call Smallwood, let him know everything's on hold for now. And why it's only on hold, not some goddamn job for Smallwood to pull without him. Get that sorted out and lie around all day, explain what's going on when Carla gets home. She finally leaves and he passes out.

He wakes sweating and shaking, scrambles out of bed, hits the floor and crawls halfway to the bathroom, gets to his feet and pushes through the door, the power of his vomit dropping him to the tile. The vomit's in front of him and beneath him. He crawls through it to the toilet, shitting hard and fast as he goes. He's still in yesterday's pants and gross as they're getting, he hopes they keep his shit off the floor. Now at least his hands are on the toilet rim and some of the puke's in the bowl. He bucks back and forth, grips the rim tighter, holds himself over it. What started as projectiles recedes now to spewing, the bursts of shit continual diarrhea.

He stops throwing up, crawls to the tub and leans his back against the outside of it, sits. The shit that's been behind his ass pushes up between his thighs. He pulls up his legs and faces the knees of his pants.

He sits that way an hour, eventually crawls to the toilet paper roll and unwraps the paper in wads. Picking up the biggest chunks of puke and shit from the tile, he flushes them down the toilet. He stands and undresses, turns his pants inside out and gets what he can out of there, flushes that down as well. He cleans the floor as best he can without mopping, gets into the shower.

He washes with hot water 'til it's gone, washes with cold after that. Out of the shower, clean and dry, he walks naked into the bedroom and puts on clean clothes. The shirt from before isn't so bad but it's wrapped in a towel with this morning's shit-stained pants. Fully dressed, he takes the bundle outside and throws it in the trash.

Back inside Tommy takes off his clothes and leaves

them on the floor next to the bed. His head throbs but the rest of him feels empty, still in pain but not like before. He lies on one side and in seconds falls asleep.

When he wakes it's to noises in the front of the house. Carla and Malik. She must have picked him up, although he don't know their day-to-day schedules, just that by now she's off work and they're out of school. Tommy's usually home later at night and in the morning. By then everyone's settled in or on their way out.

He stays in bed. Listening to their voices is better than getting up. No one checks on him, no one offers him dinner. Malik laughs and Carla joins him only not so loud. Still, they're too loud for when he's sleeping. They don't know he's here. He lies quiet, happy whether he hears them like this or falls asleep.

The door opens. Carla. He sits up.

"You're home?" she asks.

"Never left. Car's still in the driveway."

"Assumed you were working. Men you coulda left with have cars."

Tommy lies back down. "I'm sick. Can't work."

She steps toward the bed. "You aren't drunk?"

"Can't drink. Not for a while."

"How long?"

He closes his eyes. "I just wanna sleep."

"Here, you mean," she says. "In the bed."

"Gotta sleep."

"Don't snore." She walks away, shuts the door behind her.

It's raining. Damn near sacred moment during this California drought, which has been going on long as

Tommy can remember. Carla sleeps beside him. He wants to put an arm around her and hold her close but even if he does and she don't throw his arm aside, he don't know if they'll wind up fucking or if he'll get sick on her and all over the bed.

He looks at the bedside clock: 3:35. She'd definitely throw his arm off her, plus she'd remember this and get extra pissed the next time he tried. So he lies on his own side of the bed, alone but near her, and does nothing, like she wants. At least there's nothing to drink in the house and nowhere open to buy more. Makes it easier to lay off the booze, even though something light like a beer would do him good right now, help him get back to sleep. Fucking day shift world. Four hours you can't buy a drink and they make it in the middle of the night, right when drinking's all there is to do. He feels a light rumbling in his gut and remembers how he felt just hours ago. For once the world's stupidity is on his side.

No booze and no sleep though, and if he goes to the living room and falls asleep watching TV she'll think he was up drinking. He probably don't even get credit for not drinking today since he's sick, and she blames the sickness on how much he's been drinking.

The rumbling inside him becomes urgent and he's out of bed and into the bathroom, door shut and time to lift the toilet seat this time before hanging his head over the bowl. He vomits in bursts but not like before, not much left inside. It ends in dry heaves, like he's leftover sick. He stays hunched over the toilet, no sense going back to bed yet. Not like he's gonna sleep anyway. Or like she wants him there; she's just being nice while he's sick.

He hunches a couple minutes after the dry heaves stop, sits up at less of an angle a couple minutes and stands. Takes a minute doing that just to get used to it. Turns around and goes back to bed.

Carla mumbles, "You okay?"

"Yeah." He closes his eyes. She'd be up fast if she thought he was really sick. He gets that. He loves taking care of her but she don't let him. Hell, didn't seem she liked Rommel 'til the time he got away from her and got hit by a car. She said it was more like Rommel ran into the car. That totally made sense. Damn crazy dog wouldn't let anything run away from him if he could chase and catch it.

Rommel got some stitches and couldn't get taken outside because they'd bust open if he ran or jumped or did any of the shit he always did outside. Pits are a smart breed, don't put up with shit from no one, but in the house? Nowhere to run, must've felt like death to a dog that size. Carla took a week off from work, doped him like he was supposed to be doped and nursed him better than anyone deserved to be nursed, loved that dog in his pain though she said it was like he never felt any. Probably loved him more because of that.

Rommel was tiny when Carla and Tommy met.

She asked Tommy about the name. "Wasn't Rommel a Nazi?"

"The good Nazi. Didn't give a fuck about Hitler. He was a soldier."

Carla didn't get that. She worked in Human Services for the City of Oakland.

"You agree with all the city does?" Tommy asked. "Cops in riot gear cracking down on protestors?"

"What's that got to do with it?" She didn't wait for Tommy to answer. "What I do's different."

"Rommel killed himself to save his family from Hitler.

After he tried to kill Hitler. You better than that?"

Carla didn't answer.

"Man was a great soldier. Died trying to take out a motherfucker."

Carla settled for that reason, never seemed to accept or agree with it. Dog runs into a car and she gets all saintlike.

Now he lies beside her and it's been years and he don't know what car he gotta run into to get her to love him again.

When he wakes she's already gone. Good. Until they patch things up he hates it when she's here. And he's not as sick as yesterday, alone is good for talking business. He needs a cup of coffee and some time awake for that, and he should eat before coffee but his gut wants nothing. He gets out of bed, walks into the kitchen and starts some toast, goes to the bathroom and takes a leak, then back to the kitchen.

Two slices heavily buttered, he eats them slow and puts on water for coffee. He drinks it black. Halfway through the cup he calls Smallwood.

"You know who this is, right? That work we talked about? Gonna be a delay, the uh, sub-contractor I want ain't available right now."

"The sub—" Smallwood starts but Tommy cuts him off.

"Plans are no good too. Gimme a week, we can talk about a new blueprint."

"What's wrong with the plans?" Smallwood, like they're good and he knows it because they're his.

"Too dangerous," Tommy says. "Won't pass inspection."

47

"Who the fuck's gonna inspect? What are you talkin' about?"

Stupid motherfucker. Tommy knows guys who had their phone tapped. "Won't go into it over the phone. And don't do this without me. That makes it dangerous for you."

"You threatenin' me, Tommy?"

"You wanna have this conversation now, we meet somewhere. Not over the phone."

"Yeah," Smallwood says. "Okay. Yeah. We meet."

Okay but he sounds pissed. Tommy picks a place and Smallwood agrees. An hour. Tommy feels like shit, really don't wanna leave the house today but he ain't lettin' Smallwood go after this money on his own. Not only won't he get it but when he fucks up he blows the job for the next guy who tries. If Tommy's healthy maybe he takes Smallwood out of the picture, deals with Dunbar too. Way he feels today? Lucky if he makes Smallwood see sense. Lucky for both of 'em.

Tommy finishes his coffee, showers, puts on clean clothes and drives downtown to Mr. Wu—donuts and Chinese food. Sounds like a death trap but locals know Mr. Wu has the best pastries in the city. A mile from Oakland Chinatown with garish neon signs, the place looks like it's trying to keep customers away. But there's no parking for blocks and when Tommy finally gets inside the joint is packed. He's not surprised, takes his place at the end of the line. Maybe by the time he's served he'll be hungry. The morning toast and coffee did something to his belly but outside of discomfort, he's not sure what it means.

Smallwood walks in a few minutes later, joins him in line. "This place?"

"You never ate here?" Tommy's not surprised. Everything about Smallwood is a little off, like he's new to this, maybe new to the area.

Smallwood shakes his head.

"Look under the counter." Tommy nods at the glass display case. "Whatever you like best, Mr. Wu does better."

Smallwood's short laugh is derisive.

Tommy don't know how, but he knows he's being argued with. "I been in line five minutes. You think this crowd's here every day cuz the place looks so good from outside?"

"Looks like garbage." There's a look on Smallwood's face like he gets it. Not right away, though. And Tommy gotta work with this guy?

"If they could put a lie detector on you," Tommy says, "whatever you order I'd lay money down you get the best you ever had."

"Put your life on it?"

Tommy laughs. "Don't know where you been. Don't wanna know."

"So you're tellin' me shit you don't fuckin' know."

Tommy's voice drops to a whisper. "Like you told me you had a plan to make some money. Only you left out your plan's gonna kill somebody for sure. So the best comes out of that is a murder rap and not just for you." His voice goes back to normal. "We talk the job details at a table, alone. Not in a fuckin' line where we might bore the world."

Smallwood shuts up, his face shrinks.

They make it to the register and Tommy orders a load of pastries and a couple of coffees.

"This all your meals for the day?" Smallwood asks,

49

as they each carry a tray and a coffee.

They settle at a nearby table. "Upset stomach," Tommy says. "Bread's good. And the wife won't mind leftovers. Not these."

"So tell me," Smallwood says, "what's wrong with my plan?"

Tommy glances around but knows there's someone at every table around them. Everything they say here has to be quiet. He talks soft, hopes Smallwood gets it. Or he's gone.

"Their security outside on a Saturday night pickup?" Tommy says. "It's brutal. But there's another way. Inside. Like I said, I need another week then I got the right guys to do it. You get your share and everybody's happy. Fuck with my share? I see you thinkin' that. Stop thinkin'."

"Wasn't that," Smallwood says. "Just, what's your plan?"

"I let you know after I talk to my guy."

"Okay."

But they both know nothing's okay. This is two guys eating donuts and not trusting each other. They eat and drink coffee and the table's too quiet.

"Hey, Tommy?" Smallwood's halfway through his tray of food. "You don't move without me either."

Tommy nods, chews, and swallows. "My whole point." He picks up his coffee. "Don't add risk." He drinks, sets the cup down. "Job's risky enough."

"You gotta convince me your way's better."

Tommy farts loud. His gut feels better and he didn't shit himself. The smell's awful and the people nearby must notice but no one says a word, at least not loud enough Tommy can hear. Tommy don't look like a guy you'd say shit to. Even sick he's burly and mean and it shows.

Tommy laughs it stinks so bad. "That's how good the food is. No one skipped a bite."

Smallwood smiles. "Yeah, it's good, but Jesus, Tommy, wha'd you eat earlier? You still sick?"

"Same thing as before. Not as bad, though. Almost over it, got it under control."

"You *better* get that under control. Or they gonna start callin' you Tommy *Shits*."

Now Tommy laughs and it's like he likes this guy. And that's when things can get dangerous, when you mistake a man for your friend. "Yeah?" Tommy says, all serious. "I'd like to hear 'em say it."

"You know it don't work that way. No one says it *to* you. It's just your name on the street."

"I'd hear someone say it. And I'd take care of him so no one says it again."

Smallwood picks up something fluffy and chocolate. "But you're okay with Tommy Shakes."

"Men respect that name. So it's fine."

Smallwood chews slow. Mr. Wu's chocolate ain't something you rush through. He sets down the pastry and washes it down with coffee. "Yeah," he nods. "Man, this place is amazing."

"Everyone should know Mr. Wu. Always surprised someone don't."

Again like they're friends. Tommy don't like this. A good chance he winds up killing Smallwood. Last thing he wants is to like the guy.

"So," Smallwood says, "when're you gettin' back to me?"

"A week at most. Sooner if I can."

"That's fine. But Tommy? In case you decide to do this without me—you're bein' watched."

51

"That's fine," Tommy says. "Works both ways. Don't cross me. No one's alone in this world."

Tommy sits up in bed like he can plan this job right today. Feels like he worked enough just seeing Smallwood, don't really think he'll do much besides sit here this afternoon and sip from the can of Coke on the small bedside table. He bought a case of it so he can drink something while he don't touch what he wants. Gotta get well first. What he needs to know is whether Dunbar's loyal to Smallwood. Dunbar could help on this job however they do it. Smallwood can't.

He calls Juke. "Hey, it's me."

"Yeah?"

"That work we was lookin' at, you can make it out there a couple times for me, right? I'm still sick."

"When and what'm I lookin' at?"

"Inside. I can check the outside later."

"You buyin' me dinner?" Juke asks.

"I won't be there but yeah, you're covered."

"Looks better if I got a date."

Shoulda saw this coming. "Yeah, alright. Next two Saturdays. I get back to you with the time."

"Cover the bill," Juke says, "you can name the time."

Tommy tries to imagine the women Juke will take there on his dime. "You're on a budget, Juke. I'm payin' for dinner, not the whole night."

"Get back to me," and Juke's off the phone.

He will. He figures the night he was sick in The Manatee he was noticed, Juke wasn't. So Juke can watch the guys on the exchange as they enter and leave the restaurant. Tommy can watch from outside later on.

Sit alone in his car and watch how they leave. Then he'll know what kind of help he needs to pull the job. He hopes Dunbar's on his side but he won't need help to kill him if he ain't.

He sits there and drains that goddamn Coke, squeezes the can in his hand. It's empty and it crushes and hell, that's all he can do right now. Can't get up and recon the job, can't plan it 'til it's reconned, can't pull it 'til it's planned. Fuck he hates being sick. He belches, doesn't puke, sits in bed tired knowing he can't sleep, waits for things he can't control. The worst kind of waiting.

He sits like that a couple hours, maybe drifts off a couple times, gets up and takes a leak, walks to the kitchen and grabs another Coke from the fridge. Rommel didn't greet him when he got back from Mr. Wu, still ain't here. He checks the clock. Past four. Good. Malik musta got home and took him out. An active dog's a sane dog and last thing he needs right now is a crazy pit.

He waits in bed for Carla. Knows she ain't eager to see him but he don't give a fuck, needs to see her. Even if nothing happens. It's been a while and he misses her. He knows nothing's ever gonna be what it was and what it was is exactly what he needs.

She'll take care of him once she believes he's sick, not just drunk or hungover. And she won't offer homemade soup, she'll do better, go out for pho. A family of three can eat pretty cheap on Vietnamese takeout, and feeding a teenage boy is a good trick. She'd make it about her and Malik, and if he was too sick to join them in the kitchen he could eat in here alone. He was used to eating alone but it was usually in the living room after he got home late. If he could just get up and sit with them maybe he'd think of something to say while they talked.

"You always talk about you and what you care about," Carla musta told him a thousand times. But that's how you start conversations. It's up to the other people to chime in, talk about themselves. He wasn't raised to pry. He starts asking questions, he needs answers. He's fine with "How ya doin'?" and other stupid questions no one ever answers. Those questions ain't asked to get real answers. But Carla and Malik, they talk different, think different. They're not like his family or the people he works with. You need to ask open-ended questions she told him. He asked a question then—what did she mean? She said it was the kind of question that starts conversations, don't have a yes or no answer or an obvious direction. He tried those questions with Malik though and the boy never said shit. Just like Tommy woulda if anyone asked him something stupid like that.

Being himself ain't helping. Not with keeping his family together and not with his health. So the drinking cutback, that's a start. Maybe he'll still eat alone tonight but give it a day or two and he'll feel better. Then they can talk like a family, whatever that means, and he can get his wife and son back.

Only they ain't home yet and he don't have all night. He lies back down. It's still afternoon. Tommy falls asleep.

Tommy sits at the table for two, waits for Juke. It's a bar but they serve food. Juke ain't there yet but a waitress is, a big woman with tats on her arms.

"Would you like to see a menu?" She sets one on the table.

"Yeah. Ya got Coke in the can?"

54

"We serve it in a glass."

"Ya got it in the can, that's how I want it. And no fuckin' straws. And another menu for my friend when he gets here."

"Sure." She's no one to push around but sets another menu across from Tommy and when she comes back it's with a can of Coke.

Maybe she's reacting to him, maybe she's just doing her job. Either way Tommy likes her. "Thanks."

"Are you ready to order?"

"Some fries. My friend drinks."

She smiles at him like she don't give a fuck. She has big green eyes but dark brown hair, like a dye job. He's alright with that, just wonders. He ain't wondered about much during his marriage but the way things are going...

She walks away.

By the time Juke sits down the once overflowing plastic tray is only half-filled. The large tub of ketchup beside it is nearly empty.

"Where you fuckin' been?" Tommy says.

"A job that pays."

They sit quiet after that, Juke looking at the menu. Then just sitting until the big waitress returns.

"Hi," she says to Juke, with a smile a whole lot bigger than she gave Tommy. "You ready to order?"

Juke smiles back. "I'll take a number six, medium rare, with slaw." It's a bacon cheeseburger with whatever name the bar gave it but Juke won't call it that.

"And something to drink?"

"Fieldwork IPA. And a good single malt. You got something with Glen in the name?"

"Glenmorangie okay?"

"Yeah, one of those, neat."

55

She starts to walk away.

"Hey!" Tommy calls. "What's your name?"

The waitress looks back. "I'm Vicki."

"Hey, Vicki. Gimme the same beer he's getting. Cokes suck."

She smiles at him for the second time tonight and he buys it for the second time. She's round all over, what some people would call fat. Tommy wouldn't.

Juke's across the table and there's this weird tension. No one's made any promises so no one's fucked anyone over, but they still have to talk. It's a good room for that, drunk and loud but a lot of space between tables.

"Money's everywhere," Tommy starts, "except it ain't here. I don't get some soon, I'm gonna lose my family."

"Yeah, well, what's with that job at The Manatee?"

"I dunno, that prick Smallwood and that shit attention I got in there, that place needs some quiet."

"Yeah," Juke says, "but *when* we pull the job, what happens with Smallwood?"

Tommy raises his glass to his lips, drinks. "It ever gets quiet enough we pull the job, Smallwood goes away."

"You got other work for me?"

"Fuck." Tommy shakes his head. "Maybe we do this one sooner than I want. Don't know what I do in the meantime."

"So you don't know when."

"Three weeks soonest. You got other shit, do it now. Later, we work."

Juke looks confused. "Thought you needed money."

"Yeah." Tommy shakes his head. "When and where, though. I need money. I'll stay alive 'til I get it."

"Okay," Juke says. "But how's that work for you?"

A weird question, Tommy thinks. Like Juke likes

him. He didn't think Juke liked anyone.

"I get healthy, I find easy work. Breakin' guys' hands or somethin'. I been sick. Once I can work, I work." Tommy sips. He likes the taste, it's a reminder. "These girls you get…"

"What about 'em?"

"Any of 'em serious?"

"You care about my life now?" Juke looks around the room like someone important maybe just walked in.

"Got some shit goin' with my wife. We got a kid, you know."

"Got a couple myself," Juke says. "Pay 'em is all."

"Pay's different when you're married. And tryin' not to get divorced."

"I see who I see. Like 'em, I see 'em again. Sometimes a few times. No one lasts."

"But there's a chance."

"Married guys with problems," Juke says. "You're all fuckin' romantics."

"You ain't got problems, Juke?"

"None worth stayin' with."

Tommy holds his beer glass tight, wishes he had something stronger. Wishes he smoked but he didn't grow up that way, just a thing he killed time with when he was on junk. Outside of that, it was always easy to grab a drink and now when he needs a good one, it's a thing he won't do.

CHAPTER FIVE

After a week of staying home, Tommy goes to see Eddie. "Just a beer," he says, and he sits.

Eddie nods. "Still sick?"

"Nah, but it's too soon. Gut might not be strong yet."

"How 'bout the rest of you?"

"You offerin' work?"

"When I get my piece of the last job I gave ya."

"Ain't pulled that yet. You get a piece when I get mine. What about this one?"

"Guy I know wanted a few things done. Might still be hirin'. And I *do* get a piece. You want I should give him your number?"

"Damn right, Eddie. You're a fuckin' mind reader."

"Your mind ain't that hard. You're *always* lookin' for work."

Tommy gets the call that night, a guy named Cleotis. Cleotis wants to meet right away, names a Chinese place downtown. Tommy knows it, heads over.

A deep voice greets him as he walks in the door. "Tommy!"

Middle of the restaurant, a black guy sits alone at a

table for two. Tommy joins him.

"Sit down." The black guy don't get up.

Tommy sits. "Cleotis?"

Cleotis nods. He's bearded with round cheeks and dressed sharp, a man who lives well. "You hungry? I already ordered." He sips tea.

"Nah, I just ate."

"You know who I work for? Eddie tell you?"

"Eddie don't even tell me your name, found out when you called."

Cleotis nods again. "I work for a serious man. Name of Little Bessie."

Little Bessie was Gino Bessanelli. His operations were widespread along the West Coast, but more L.A. than the Bay Area. Still, a man like that has his hand in a lot of things. Someone you don't fuck with.

Anyone wonders why a guy big as Gino gets called Little Bessie don't know his old man. That's all it was, there was already a Big Bessie then his boy come along. Little Bessie was huge but that don't mean a thing; there's a boy and there's his old man.

"What's the job?" Tommy asks.

"Little Bessie has a guy he don't like. Don't want him gone, wants him scared. Guy owes Bess some money. Bess wants the man to feel his pain."

"Tell me about the guy."

Cleotis angles his head to one side. "Whaddaya think? Guy owes money. He acts like he don't remember. Give him a reminder is all."

Hurt a guy. Easy work, exactly what Tommy needs.

"Just need to know who the fuck is he, where I find him."

* * *

The guy who owes Little Bessie is in Oakland, and Little Bessie don't have regulars up here. A job comes up, he looks around. Finds someone got nothin' to do with him, he's good.

This guy needs to be hurt. Tommy needs to get paid, so he got no problem with that. He's *glad* this fuck needs to get hurt outside Little Bessie's usual turf.

The fuck is named Mitchell, divorced and lives alone in a shithole apartment. Not a total shithole, he works, but he got bills like everyone else and he got child support like a lotta everyone else and he got gambling debts to cover but he can't pay and now he's fucked and that's good for Tommy. That's life, one guy loses and another wins. Trick is when the guy starts losing, be there to help him lose more.

Mitchell works days. Tommy shows up at night, eight o'clock. Mitchell's on the third floor. Tommy picks another apartment on that floor, presses the buzzer. "Hey, it's me, Mitch, forgot my key, wouldya buzz me in." He does that on four different apartments and he's about to do the fifth when the front door buzzes. He opens it and walks in, glad people are fucking idiots.

Tommy takes the elevator to three, walks down the hall and knocks on Mitchell's door, solid but not loud enough to sound pissed.

"Yeah?" says a voice behind the door, not real close.

"Yo, Mitch. Take a peek, see I'm alone. Little Bessie sent me. Open up or the next guy's an army."

It takes a minute but there's fumbling at the door chain then the various locks are undone and the door opens. Mitchell's stepped back a ways so he's not right in front of Tommy when he walks in the door. But he's alone, and that's enough. He holds a pistol pointed at the floor but that don't mean shit besides common sense.

"You don't need the pistol, Mitch. And you don't need to have money yet. I ain't here to kill or collect. I'm here to talk. We can sit down, have a drink if you got."

Mitchell looks ready to shit like Tommy was shitting two weeks ago, only Mitchell's sickness got him into Little Bessie instead of just booze. Shaking, he raises his pistol at Tommy. He looks about to cry. "I can't trust nobody."

"Put that fuckin' pistol down, man. I ain't no enforcer. I'm here to explain things."

"Bullshit. They only send enforcers."

"They send someone to kill you," Tommy says, "you won't see him. It's like the mosquito. You know the mosquito? Fuckin' pain in the ass, but the one that buzzes? That's the male, it don't bite. The female bites, don't make a fuckin' sound. That's how it is with Little Bessie. You hear a damn thing, it might keep you awake, but you hear nothin'? That's when you're dead. I'm here to talk, and you don't drop that fuckin' pistol, the next thing you hear is nothin'. And you hear it forever."

Mitchell still holds the pistol but his arm shakes. Tommy walks straight at him and Mitchell brings the gun up but Tommy's hand is on his wrist. Tommy yanks Mitchell's arm up and the gun fires one round into the ceiling. Tommy swings Mitchell's arm up higher, then hard backward until it's behind him. Tommy moves behind him and yanks the arm up until it cracks. Mitchell screams and the pistol hits the floor. Tommy steps forward and grabs Mitchell by the shirt collar, pulls him to his knees. Mitchell's in tears, his teeth jammed together.

"You owe Little Bess. You pay Little Bess." Tommy

drops him and the second Mitchell lands Tommy punches him in the gut. Mitchell lurches forward, looks up at Tommy.

"You pay Little Bess," Tommy says, and steps behind Mitchell. "Or this trip's like a picnic." He throws a hard right to Mitchell's kidney and sends him sprawling forward. He lies there and Tommy kicks him in the ribs, rolls him over with the heel of his boot and kicks him in the ribs again. "Pay Little Bessie."

Mitchell gags, gasps, coughs.

Tommy kicks him in the mouth and Mitchell's blood hits the carpet. "Pay Little Bessie." He walks out of the apartment to the sound of sirens, but no one in this part of Oakland's dumb enough to look outside their door right after a gunshot.

It's Saturday night and Tommy pulls up outside The Manatee, Juke with him.

"Your show," Juke says. "How we split up?"

Tommy lights a cigarette. He hasn't smoked much since he was sick, but right now it's in his hand and he's smoking, not even a choice. "You got smokes?"

"What, you low? Ya got one in your mouth."

Tommy exhales a cloud. "There's two places we can watch the front. I'll be in the alley across the street. You gotta be in this bar over here." He points down the street with his cigarette. "Four doors down. Don't need to come out at all 'til I text you. Then you step outside to smoke while the deal gets done."

"And I see something you don't?"

"The broads might like ya cuz you're pretty. I don't give a fuck. Ya know yer fuckin' job, and maybe you see somethin'. We gonna do this three times before the job goes down. We talk after every time. I better know how to pull this off by then."

Juke nods. "Yeah, I got smokes."

"Drink slow. They ain't even here yet."

"Hard to set up in the alley if they were, right?" Juke smiles and walks to the bar.

Tommy likes the kid, he picks up shit quick. This job? Tommy's not sure, but he's doing it. He could lie to Smallwood but for now he's gonna tell him the truth, just leave out some details. He'll meet Smallwood and Dunbar separate, let 'em know the job's on for some time in December. Even if they ain't in it.

Tommy gets home past midnight, sits on the couch. Beer bottle in one hand, he pets Rommel with the other. The money that changed hands at The Manatee tonight was all in one large suitcase. Easy to carry once taken, that's the good news. But two guys brought the suitcase out, one carrying and one behind, and they were met out front by two guys, plus there were two in the waiting car. So, six guys to take out if they do it right outside, four if they somehow deal with just the guys in the car after the case gets handed off. And inside the club there's more guys, but sometimes the number don't mean as much as who they are. Tommy recognized one of the pickup guys. He works for Joey Lee. This place ain't supposed to have no protection.

More money if they pull the job on a Saturday but easier to pull it on a Friday. A whole lot easier if the place is running without permission, like Smallwood said. If Joey Lee's backing the place, it's a whole other deal. He needs to pull this job. But he sure as fuck has to find out if that one guy picking up the money means this is a Joey Lee joint. And why else would anyone who works for Joey get in on this? Suicide to cross him. Of course, the world's filled with suicidal men.

Tommy hopes he hasn't become one.

He wakes up in bed when Carla gets up, keeps his eyes closed. On the verge of sleep again but while his thinking sort of works he wonders if he and Carla are getting along now, if what she wants from him is no longer different from what he wants from her. And if everything between them is good now and they'll fuck tonight. But he knows drifting off that everything isn't good, and even if they fuck it'll just be one of those rare moments when she believes in him. She always thinks later that he fooled her.

Maybe that's what he does. His half-sleep has him thinking too much. He wants to be away from all this until he's done with it, when she sees he's stopped being a fuckup. He's gonna pull this fucking job at The Manatee and on top of what he made on the Little Bess job, he's looking like steady money. He could always do the work. People see him not fucking up he gets a lot more jobs.

Tommy wakes up. Carla's gone and he sits in bed with his arms wrapped around his knees like that's how he sleeps. But he's up now and in the kitchen making coffee. No one's home and he wears just his boxers. Who the fuck's that guy he recognized? Where's he rank? Is he crossing Joey Lee or is Joey in on this shit?

If The Manatee's unprotected like Smallwood said, then maybe Joey's guy just saw a chance to make something extra. Except the guy's not ripping off the place, he's working for it. Tommy needs to find out who's fucking over who here. So he knows who he's fucking over when he rips them off. So he knows how to defend himself when the job's over.

He drinks coffee with the TV on, paces behind the couch. Rommel sits in front of it, looks up at him. Hell of a time not to be drinking whiskey but it's too soon. Too soon in the day, too soon after being sick, too soon to know if there's a reason for it. It means he has to make phone calls, but who's he gonna ask? Who's in with Joey Lee's crowd? Hell, he don't even know the name of the guy he wants to ask about. And no one can know why he's asking. Word can't get back to anyone. Sure as hell not Joey Lee.

No one but Smallwood. Tommy puts on the pot for more coffee and picks up his phone.

Outdoor tables at a Grand Avenue café near Lake Merritt, no one on the sidewalk but a lot of cars in the street. People will walk past once in a while, but only on their way to or from one of the other food or drink places around here. Mid-afternoon in November, the Oakland weather don't call for a leather jacket but Tommy wears one anyway. Smallwood wears a black sport coat and pants almost as dark. He sits across the table with a coffee.

Tommy's waiting with his beer. "Smallwood." He takes a drink.

"Tommy."

"I'm looking at this job and maybe a problem comes up."

"Problems always come up, Tommy, you know that."

Tommy looks over his glass at Smallwood, wonders if the man has any idea what he's talking about, if he ever worked a rip-off. "There's four guys do the pickup. I need their names."

It takes a second, but Smallwood gets it. "And you need me to get them for you? Why can't you do it?"

Tommy shakes his head. "I'm street level on this, you're background. I can't be seen looking into it."

"I can't either." Smallwood's grip tightens on his coffee. Tommy would love to play cards with this guy.

"So don't. You're background. That's what background does."

"I also planned the job."

"With your plan, people die. Maybe us, maybe them." He shrugs. "I don't like it either way. You want a piece of this, get me the names."

"Want a piece?" Smallwood looks around them, knows his voice has risen. A couple of people are looking his way. His voice lowers, stays insistent. "This is *my* job. You ain't in this without me."

"Now it's the other way 'round. Get me those names. Then tell Dunbar the job's on. Once I get those names."

"Okay. But what's so special 'bout the names?"

Tommy leans back, drinks from his beer. "You just rippin' off a restaurant, or you got someone special in mind?"

"What are you talkin' about?"

"There's more guys pickin' up than you said. Makes the job harder if we take 'em outside. I gotta know how hard."

Smallwood nods, like that explains it. Then his face goes blank. "You're holdin' somethin' back."

"Everyone holds somethin' back."

"You gotta tell me. We're partners."

"I'll tell ya when I know. When it has anything to do with the plan. Ain't gonna tell ya what I fuckin' guess."

No idea what kind of names Smallwood's gonna come up with or where he's gonna get 'em. Tommy knows who to go to for information in Oakland. The one reliable source they say no one can touch, he has too much power of his own. And he can usually be found not far from here.

Tommy drives a couple miles and parks, walks a few blocks to Starbucks. He sees his guy right away at an outdoor table: short and skinny with glasses and almost bald, reading a newspaper, nothing else in front of him but a coffee.

Tommy walks up to the table. "Carelli?"

"What do you want? Keep it quiet and quick. Sit down."

Tommy sits.

"Who are you?"

"They call me Tommy Shakes."

"Shakowski, right?"

Tommy's surprised. "How? No one calls me that."

"You got busted once, made the papers. I read a lot of papers. And talk to way too many people. It's all up here." Carelli taps himself on the side of the head. "Terrible thing, a photographic memory. It's fucking awful and goddamn useful. Now. What do you want?"

"A restaurant called The Manatee. They run a sports book in back. Saturday nights they run the money from the restaurant to somewhere else. Four guys pick up. I need their names. And who owns the place."

Tommy says this and it better be true Carelli don't sell no one out. He pretty much confessed he's pulling the job.

Carelli looks at Tommy like they're talking about the weather. "What's the information worth to you?"

"I can get you two large. Tonight if you want."

Carelli smiles. It ain't pleasant. "I don't work nights. And the price is five. Come back to me when you have it."

"Five for a few names?"

"You can always borrow the rest. I'm sure you know people who lend money."

He says it like he knows Tommy does collections for loan sharks. "Two now, the rest later, but I need the names right away."

"How much later?"

"A few weeks. Before Christmas."

Carelli drinks coffee, sets it down. "Be here this time tomorrow. With cash. And the five later is on top of the two. And Tommy? Don't fuck with me on the rest. I get it by Christmas."

Tommy hears the words and knows Carelli's as dangerous as any gang he has information on. He sits out here and does business in public because he's got his own men. And he's probably crazy.

CHAPTER SIX

Tommy's home early, Carla and Malik in the kitchen. Tommy walks up behind Carla where she stands at the stove, walks up loud enough she won't be surprised and kisses her on the cheek. He steps away without grabbing her, much as he wants to. Don't want to give her an excuse to get pissed off.

Malik's at the table, a schoolbook open in front of him.

"Hey, whatcha studyin'?"

Malik don't look up. "Algebra."

"How's that?"

Malik glances at him. "Okay."

"Yeah, wish I could help with that one but I don't know shit about algebra."

Malik don't answer. Carla don't even say anything about Tommy swearing to him. He's fifteen, he hears worse.

"You have a good day at school?"

"It's okay."

A two-word sentence. The kid's really opening up. "You gotta do this now? I thought we might catch a movie or somethin'."

Malik glances at his dad. "I have a midterm tomorrow." His eyes return to the book.

"Okay." Tommy looks at Carla, her back to him. "How 'bout you? What's your day like?"

"Nothing special. Long day at work, been cooking for Malik since I got home."

"He eat okay?"

"He's a fifteen-year-old boy. He *always* eats okay."

"But did he get enough?" When Tommy was fifteen he always wanted more. "He gets done studyin', we could go for ice cream or somethin'."

"That's up to him," Carla says. "You're the one needs to watch what you eat."

Tommy glares at her but there's not much hostile about her words. A little more fact than he wants to hear right now. Bad enough he's cutting back on drinking when he's got all this work. He don't say a word about that, looks at Malik instead. "You wanna go out when you're done?"

"I'm not hungry."

Tommy goes to the fridge and grabs a beer.

"You know what that means," she says, as he steps to the drawer with the bottle opener.

"What?" He has no idea.

"You drink, you snore."

He opens the bottle. "It's only a beer." He tips his head back, takes a long swallow.

"You wanna talk about this in here?"

"Don't wanna talk at all." He walks out of the kitchen.

Carla makes sure she's turned off the stove and follows him into the living room.

Tommy stands in front of the couch. "You gonna say I can't sleep in my own bed if I have one goddamn beer."

Carla stops a few feet from him. "You can't sleep in

mine. Bad enough you don't know anything about me or Malik, you don't do a damn thing around the house, now you wanna snore and keep me awake?"

"No one *wants* to snore."

"You know I can't sleep when you snore and you know you snore when you drink. And you say you care about me but you're gonna drink and wanna sleep in my bed?"

"Our bed."

"Our bed 'til you get so selfish I can't sleep."

"I'm not drinkin'. It's a beer."

"You snore when you drink. Maybe you sleep well enough to do the shit you do. I work in Human Services. I gotta sleep better than that."

Tommy sits on the couch and drinks. He's not gonna win this argument and he loves her too much to hit her. She hardly ever drinks, she don't know the difference. Jesus, he'll never get laid at this rate.

Carla stares at him, worse than when she yells. She keeps staring, he keeps drinking.

"You gotta make up your mind what you want from us, Tommy." She walks back into the kitchen.

Tommy finishes his beer, puts his empty on the table in front of him, and leaves the house.

A different bar tonight. He don't want Eddie to see him when he feels like this. It might matter next time he needs work.

There's one pretty woman alone on a corner stool. Tommy figures that means she's married. A single broad looks like that don't come into a place like this. Not alone. Unless she's trying to get back at a guy. Then it's the same as she's married.

Tommy don't mind helping with revenge.

He strolls down that way, past a lot of empty seats. This place'll be jumpin' in an hour or two. Not yet.

Ten years younger than him, about Carla's age and almost as pretty. "Buy ya a drink?"

She blinks at him, she's been here a while. "Thought you'd never ask." She talks slow, manages not to slur the words.

The bartender's already headed his way. Tommy looks at the brunette beside him. "What're you havin'?"

"Tequila Sunrise."

Late for that, Tommy thinks, but maybe that's what she's been doin' all day. Hell of a tolerance if that's the case.

"A Tequila Sunrise for the lady," Tommy says when the bartender gets there, "and a Racer 5 for me."

"Ain't got Racer. Want Lagunitas?"

"Sure." Wasn't like it was hard to get a good IPA in California, definitely not around here.

The bartender turns away and Tommy looks at the brunette. "I'm Tommy."

"Amanda," she says and holds out her hand. Tommy shakes it, assumes she's lying about her name. He don't have to about his; she's drunk.

"You don't come here much, do ya?" Tommy asks.

Amanda laughs. "You walked around the obvious way of sayin' that."

"What?"

"Come here often? The opposite of what you said."

Tommy shakes his head. Maybe she's smart, maybe she's drunk, maybe both. Whatever it is, she don't think like anyone normal. "Just wonderin' if you're new in town."

She laughs harder. It takes a while before she stops. "Now you're talkin'."

Tommy has no idea what she's talking about. Don't care much either. She got curves. "I just mean," Tommy says, trying to figure out what he was saying if it wasn't a question, "this ain't a place where pretty young women show up alone. Don't wanna pry, just lookin' if there's a obvious reason."

"Snuck in a compliment. You're good, Tommy. So tell me why pretty young women don't come here alone."

Tommy shrugs. "The crowd, when it gets here. Right now it's just guys came straight from work, all they're gonna do is bury themselves in booze. Done that myself a while back, didn't work so good. The guys who cause trouble show up the next couple hours. Guys who drink whiskey right outside the factory, save money on the hard stuff before they hit the bars. And they always hit bars like this. Hit each other too. If they're dumb enough, they try to hit me. And that kinda guy sees a woman after a few drinks? You don't wanna be that woman."

The bartender brings their drinks. Amanda is on hers in an instant, takes a sip through the straw and sets down the glass almost as fast. "You don't know what kinda woman I want to be."

"Yeah, you might be stupid but you don't seem like it. Maybe you got some reason to hate yourself so you want some guy to punish you. Is that you? The way you're drinkin' I thought maybe you like to punish yourself."

Amanda sips from her straw. "You're smarter than you look. You think I'm dumber?"

"Just sayin', I know what it's like when things are

73

bad and a few drinks sound like a way out. I'm here for a few tonight."

"Punishing yourself?"

"Just windin' down."

"Right," she says. "Me too. No reason to think I want to be hurt. By anyone."

Tommy looks at her. She's pretty, that's why he's talking to her. Something else about her he likes but damned if he knows what. He's out because Carla, he drinks because Carla. For a night he'd like it not to be Carla. "Ain't none a my business why you're here. Just thought you should know who else is gonna be."

"I know who goes to bars."

Tommy shakes his head. "Some people think they go to bars, they know why everyone goes to bars. Ain't like that. Lotta reasons."

Amanda laughs. "Don't know who I look like to you. My folks owned a bar. Saw it all as a kid, like a movie on why not to drink. Every asshole in the world rolls in, rolls up his sleeves, and fights every other asshole. If you're lucky. The others use weapons, they kill and they rape. Seen it all, from way too close. You gonna tell me what I don't know?"

Tommy grins in surprise, takes a drink. "Ain't tellin' you shit. But you know and you're still here."

He don't ask the question. She answers. "They can fuck with me if they want, they can kill me. Already been fucked, already lived. But I don't believe they're gonna do it. Don't believe anyone makes anything worse than it is now."

Tommy drinks again. This broad. "What's bad now?"

Amanda shakes her head. "You don't want me drunk enough to answer that."

Tommy talks soft. "I just wanna know."

"It's private. Lay off."

There's finality to that. If Tommy was standing he'd probably step back. Instead he leans in, like a boxer who's been hit and knows he has to fight inside. But he keeps his mouth shut.

"You gonna say somethin'?" she asks.

"You gonna be okay?"

"Tonight?"

He nods.

"I'm gonna be okay no matter what. Anyone bothers me? Worry about them."

She don't look tough but when she says it, he buys it. Growing up in bars makes sense. Knowing what these guys are like makes sense too, but every guy's different. Someone's gonna be the guy she can't handle, he just don't know when. But tonight, he's here.

"I'm stayin' here. You walk off with one a them, it's on you."

"You gonna protect me?" Her smile says she don't need him. Says he needs her.

Tonight maybe he does. "Gonna drink with you. That makes you safe, then yeah."

"We got a whole conversation based on you think I need protection."

Tommy sighs. "Just bein' friendly." She's starting to bug him.

"When you buy me a drink, that's friendly. When you say I need help, that's an insult."

"What?"

"Like I'm a woman and you're a man and if some asshole wants to rape me, I need a man. Whose side you on, Tommy?"

"What the fuck?" Tommy says. "Just gave you a warning. You don't need it, fine, you said that."

"You think I'm weak cuz I'm a woman, right?"

"Thought you might need help is all."

"And now you think what? I'm some psycho dyke bitch?"

"Nah," Tommy says. "I just think you're pretty. And pissed."

"Hmmm." Amanda sips from her straw. "That's really what you think, isn't it?"

Tommy's glad he don't go up against women on jobs. She just made him say what's in his head. He finishes his beer, looks at her glass. Almost empty. The bartender's right there. "Another round."

The bartender nods, finishes the rest of his business this end of the bar, turns away.

"You know, Tommy," she says, "you're not a total asshole."

Those might be the nicest words he hears tonight. "Like I said, just windin' down."

And now this crazy woman has a hand next to his on the bar. His hand covers hers. It's warm. Now he's with Amanda and none of that shit he warned her about is gonna happen. While she's with him. But what he cares about is she didn't resist when he took her hand. Their drinks arrive and they drink with their free hands, don't let go of each other. This night, maybe, has a chance.

A couple more rounds and his arm is around her. Talk's been quiet, like the big things were said early. Words don't feel like they matter anymore. But there's a few.

"Let's get outta here," he says.

"I have a husband to go home to."

"And I have a wife." Tommy holds up his left hand, wiggles his fingers like he's showing off his ring. "We ain't home yet."

"Hell," she says, "you ain't even made it to first base."

"Ah Jesus. You gonna act like this now?"

"What, like we meant something to each other? You want your three drinks back?"

Tommy looks at his beer, wonders if it's enough tonight. It should be. This bitch just gave him hope.

"You want," he says, "I leave you to these pricks just now walkin' in. You deal with who you like."

She looks past him. "I don't like anyone. Least of all my husband. Still going home when I leave here."

"So. You wanna do somethin' here?"

Amanda almost spits. "Shit. With you? Idiot. I wanna drink. Stick around a little, maybe I say when I'm gonna be here again."

Tommy's beer is near full. He takes a long drink. "I can drink and not get laid at home. A lot cheaper than here."

"Fine. Won't see ya next time."

The bar's getting crowded and it's almost all guys. Tommy wasn't lying about them drinking before they came here. He leaves her now, she's gonna have shit to deal with. He stands and picks up his half-full beer. "See ya."

Tommy works his way through the crowd halfway to the wall. Amanda looks surprised, watches him walk away. Like he has time for bullshit that costs him money. He has two meetings tomorrow, Smallwood in the morning and Carelli in the afternoon. Well, morning might be an exaggeration, but it'll be before the meet with Carelli.

A couple guys move in next to Amanda, one on each

side. Amanda's near the wall so the guy on that side leans on it behind her like they're all buddies. Tommy sips slow and watches them work. Too far away to hear what gets said, and she looks in control at first. But they have her surrounded, and he knows they're shitheels. *He* wouldn't talk to most of the guys come in here, no way a woman wants to.

Tommy keeps drinking slow, watching over the lip of the bottle. So he sees when the guy closer to him puts a hand on the back of her neck. She shakes it off and turns on her stool to face him. The guy behind her grabs her shoulder like he's gonna calm her down, straighten her out.

Tommy takes a couple steps forward but don't get close enough to do anything about it, just enough to gauge how hard it is to move through the crowd. He's several feet away and none of the three has a clear view of him. The guys are watching her and she's turning to get the one guy's hand off her shoulder then the other guy's hand is on her neck again.

Her mouth opens wide like she's yelling, but the place is packed and her voice don't carry. The bartender isn't close and there's no security and none of the customers give a fuck. Then the guy closer to Tommy kisses her and she tries to stand and the guy behind her pushes her back onto her stool.

Tommy's elbows are out and he clears a path and he's behind the closest guy, grabs his hair from the back and slams his forehead off the bar. The guy's bleeding and swings while the other guy says "What the fuck." The swing's off-balance and grazes Tommy's chest as he steps behind Amanda, wraps his arm around the other guy's neck, and pushes him against the wall. He chokes him there a second and knows the guy with the bloody forehead's gathered strength by now. He comes off the bar at Tommy from behind, but there's a reason Tommy hung onto his near empty bottle. He drops his head and swings the bottle at an angle between a hook and an uppercut that catches the guy across the cheek and sends him back into the crowd. Tommy glares back toward the wall and the man he pinned there scoots away. The bartender's yelling and grabbing a phone as Tommy takes Amanda by the elbow and with the other hand raises his bottle and walks past the first guy, who's being propped up by the crowd, but he won't let them push him back to his feet, the fear is in his eyes.

The crowd parts for Tommy and he gets Amanda to the parking lot, walks her to his car and opens the passenger door. She gets in.

He sits down beside her. They're both drunk. "You drive here?"

She shakes her head. "Uber."

Tommy smiles. "Shouldn't do that." He starts the engine. "Leaves a record where you been."

He's drunk but he's beer drunk and he just committed assault and battery, assault with a deadly weapon, god knows what else. He needs to get the fuck away from here without driving crazy, take his chances on a goddamn DUI.

A couple blocks from the bar, Amanda starts the conversation. "We ain't goin' to a hotel."

Tommy smiles. "So I just pull over?"

"I toldja, I'm goin' home to my husband."

"Jesus, I saved your life back there."

"And my pussy's a reward cuz you're less of a dick than those assholes?"

79

"I *think*," Tommy says, "it's normal gratitude. You already like me."

"There's plenty people I like I never sleep with. And fuck you anyway, Tommy. You coulda stopped those guys sooner. You watched, waited 'til you'd have to beat the hell out of 'em to help. For all I know, you're some fuckin' psycho."

"Yeah, but *this* fuckin' psycho saved you."

"Drive me home, psycho."

Tommy drives slow. The road ain't busy. "Maybe I just pull over up ahead a little. Where no one sees us."

"Do it that way," Amanda says, "nothin' happens unless it's rape. And you rape me, you never see me again."

"Who says I want to?"

"Who says I don't want to do it more than once if it doesn't happen that way? And really, Tommy, you think I don't have a pistol aimed at your gut right now?"

He glances down. Amanda has her left hand in her purse between them.

"Where's your place and how close is safe to drop you? And how do I see you again?"

"Give it a week then go back to the same place."

"And you're there?"

"If I am, you got a chance."

"What about now?"

"You get gut shot."

Tommy pulls over. "You good at walkin' from here?"

It's six blocks from the address she gave. Amanda opens her door, gets out. "Try me next week." She shuts the door and walks away.

CHAPTER SEVEN

Another public place, another meeting with Smallwood. A bar this time, early afternoon. Tommy was up late and slept lousy on the couch, not so great after Carla told him to get in the bed either. By now he's alright. He's on his second beer; the first one didn't count, was just a return to reality. This one feels like a beer and he's in the place a half hour before Smallwood shows, sees him at his table, nods and walks to the bar. He comes back with a beer and sits.

"Wha'd ya find out?" Tommy asks. "About the guys pickin' up."

Smallwood slides his hand across the bare wood table. "One of 'em's maybe wrong."

"Wrong how?" This is the answer Tommy needs. This and who else is in it.

"The guy's named Fang. He works for Joey Lee."

Tommy sits back fast like he's surprised. "Joey's in this."

"I doubt it. Fang's the only Chinese on the pickup."

"You doubt? You don't know? You're my fuckin' contact on this job. You were maybe gonna turn me over to Joey Lee?"

Smallwood shakes his head fast. "Didn't say I'm

81

done checkin' on it. This is what I know since yesterday."

"Yeah, but you had this job checked out forever when you came to me. Then you have some idiot plan that no way I'm gonna work on, so now you're not in the action—you settin' me up?"

Smallwood's turn to pull back. "Fuck no, Tommy. I didn't know, okay? I'll keep checking."

"You know who Joey Lee *is*, right? You know he runs half this county?"

"I'm not an idiot, Tommy. I toldya I'm checking this out."

Tommy shakes his head, picks up his beer. "Jesus. Now you're gonna check. If I didn't say anything you'd wait 'til I was locked up. What's your fuckin' problem, Smallwood? Who's the other guys? Names, asshole."

"Justin Fang. That's Joey Lee's guy. The other three are black."

This much Tommy knows.

Smallwood reaches into a pants pocket and Tommy puts a hand inside his coat. "Chill, Tommy. I'm just getting the names."

Tommy's eyes roll. "You ain't memorized 'em yet? What'd you do last night? Make a phone call and watch a ball game?"

"Fuck you, Tommy. Let me get the list out."

Tommy holds his beer in one hand and his pistol in the other. The pistol's under his coat and there's no way Smallwood makes him bring it out. Also no way he lets Smallwood think he won't.

A scrap of paper in his hand, Smallwood reads. "Percelle Rakim, Rashad Williamson, Taurean Wolf."

"Put the paper in front of me."

Smallwood does.

"Man," Tommy says when he's done reading. "I knew they were black when I saw 'em. Didn't know they'd sound so black."

Smallwood grips his glass, don't pick it up. "You can keep that."

"No fuckin' shit." Tommy drinks.

Smallwood drinks too.

"Still a gun on ya," Tommy says when he sets his beer down. One hand stays inside his jacket. "Always gonna be a gun on ya. Cuz now ya fucked me. Joey Lee's maybe in this and you say the place ain't protected. But this guy Fang, you don't know how high up he is, do ya?"

"I told you," Smallwood says, "I'm still lookin' into it."

"You look slow, it's the same as murder to me. I get fucked, I'm lookin' for the guy who fucked me."

Smallwood shakes his head fast like this is where Tommy's gonna shoot him.

Tommy's smile grows. "So, you got names. That it? I wanna know who all these motherfuckers are. What's Fang to Joey, is Joey in on this—and yeah, that one matters most—and who the fuck these other assholes are. Who they're with, what they done time for, what they ain't done time for. You ever done a job, assfuck? Cuz all these motherfuckers are paid to protect the money we're gonna take. And don't go light on any of this. Even if it has to do with Joey, I'm takin' this motherfucker. Fuck with what's at stake here, you're dead. That's what you need to remember, cocksuck. You gonna give me everything on everyone. Joey's stake, everyone's stake. And don't cross me on this shit. I got backup and they know your name. I get dead, you get dead a whole lot slower. You're callin' me tomorrow."

Tommy stands, drains the half of his beer remaining,

keeps his eyes on Smallwood and a hand in his jacket as he walks out.

He goes to Carelli. Almost five o'clock. The sun's gone soon and there's a chill, at least by California standards. Tommy's here from birth, he pulls his coat tight, but the weather's not his main concern. Carelli's at his usual table, Tommy sees him from the sidewalk. Carelli's gonna know more than Smallwood. What matters is if he contradicts him.

Tommy steps over.

Carelli looks up. "Just goin' home. Make it worth my time."

Tommy pulls a thick envelope from his pocket, sets it in front of Carelli.

"You wanted to know who owns the place. Sounds like a law firm: Gerson, Poole, and McCarthy. Crooks, sure, but all white collar 'til now. Businessmen looking for adventure."

"Who does the pickup?"

"You takin' notes? I got full bios. Write nothin' down."

"Gimme the names. Details later."

"Justin Fang, Percelle Rakim, Taurean Wolf, Rashad Williamson. The guys with the black names, they're all independents. Fang works for Joey Lee, but this looks like it got nothing to do with Joey. Fang's fairly high up, he goes for money Joey don't know about? Stupid. Like, dead stupid.

"Think on it. So far, it's quiet. Maybe Joey ain't in it now, but he gets fucked on this? He gets loud. Joey's young, but he grew up right. He kills what's in his way. Either Fang's a dead man or anyone who knocks off this joint's a dead man. You better hope it's Fang. Cuz you owe me five by Christmas. Two ways I take payment. Cash and flesh."

So it's Joey Lee or Carelli. Someone might kill him no matter what he does. The good news: he has to do something.

"Whattaya mean," Tommy says, "it looks like it got nothin' to do with Joey. Does it or don't it?"

"He's not in it. At all. There's a day he's gonna know, so don't wait forever, but right now? Not a fuckin' clue."

"And you're sure."

"I tell someone somethin', I'm always sure. Now get the fuck outta here. Next time I see you I want money."

Tommy's home. Carla and Malik will be here soon. He had his beers at the bar but he hasn't had a drink since and he's loaded the kitchen table with Chinese takeout, minus the order of chow fun he pretty much inhaled. The meals with loads of vegetables are best when you're trying to get in shape, but when stress kicks in: noodles. Chinese, Italian, don't fucking matter, something in there fills more than the gut.

It's seven and they ain't home yet and he don't know why not. He's trying not to eat more until they get here but he didn't get any booze, trying to be what Carla wants, so he grabs one of the boxes of egg rolls and takes it to the couch, turns on the TV, sets the egg rolls on the table.

He gets out his phone, makes a call.

Juke picks up. "Yeah?"

"We're gonna do that job we talked about. There's

somethin' I want you to look into. You free—" Tommy looks at his watch. Seven oh five. "—about nine?"

"I'm free now. You wanna meet?"

"Alright. Same place as last time. Fifteen minutes."

"You mean the bar? Last time was the restaurant."

"Yeah, the bar." Tommy ends the call, sends Carla a text letting her know dinner's on the table, and takes off.

He's at the bar in twenty minutes, faster than Juke gets there. He likes to be the first one at places. Tommy takes a stool at the bar and turns his back to the bartender, faces the door. It's beer, it can only be sipped so slow, he's on his second when Juke walks in.

Juke greets him with a handshake, orders a beer and a shot. Juke waits until Tommy pays and they leave their stools, take a table.

They sit. "Nice suit." It's dark and sleek and about a million times nicer than what anyone else in the bar is wearing. "You trying to get mugged?"

"They can fuck with me if they want." Juke shrugs. "I got a date later. So we're doin' this now."

The fingers between Tommy's right thumb and pinkie play three quick beats, tap tap tap. "I need you to look into a possible problem. There's a guy works for Joey Lee on the pickup."

"Ah fuck. And Joey?"

"He don't know yet. Can't let him find out."

"And you're payin' me to look at the guy?"

"Justin Fang. One large to look at him. And find out if he's crossing Joey or might bring him in later. If he might bring him in, I assume you want more when we pull the job."

Juke drinks his shot. "You wanna pull this even if Joey's involved? What kinda shit you in?"

"I gotta do this. The rest don't matter."

"To you."

"If Joey's in it and you want out, understood. Just don't give me any bullshit. If Fang might bring Joey in or not, I gotta know."

"I'll do that much," Juke says. "But it ain't my goal in life to fuck with Joey Lee." He brushes his knuckles down the front of his suit coat. "I got reasons to be alive."

"We all got our reasons, Juke."

"You been a reliable guy, Tommy. I'll look into it. No promises past that."

"One more thing, Juke. That guy Dunbar, works for Smallwood? I need his number."

Juke nods. Both men drink, neither talks. A quiet night at the bar—everything Tommy could ask for. He gets up and buys another round, but when he walks back to the table with two beers and a shot, Juke ain't here no more.

This is as good as things get right now. Total shit everywhere he turns. He drinks from his beer, then he drinks from Juke's, then he drinks Juke's shot and it ain't enough and he goes to the bar and buys another. And another. He drinks a while. He misses work being a simpler thing. He misses Carla.

But it's another night not to hurry home. Chinese takeout won't make up for him walking in drunk, especially if it's early and Malik's still up. Another night on the couch with Rommel, another early morning ordered into bed. Sleep will be nightmares and being awake will be the same. He keeps ordering shots. He'll cab home when they close or kick him out, whatever happens first. It's one thing if he dies crossing Joey Lee because he's taking care of his family. He dies driving home drunk, maybe takes someone with him? Ain't just him dying then, it's every-thing about him, what Carla thinks of him.

The cab comes and Tommy gives the name of a down-town hotel. Fuck Carla and his having to get off the couch. He's gonna hurt in the morning and she can think what she wants why he didn't come home. She wants him around, she has to want him. None of this sleep on the couch, get off the couch shit. What's he, the fucking dog?

In the hotel he sleeps on a decent-size bed. Alone, but he sleeps. Ain't like he's fucking Carla anyway. And it feels like she and Malik have adjusted to it being the two of them, him out of the picture. He's the one who feels something's missing. He wakes alone on that goddamn bed and alone's how he always wakes so that part's good. The pain from all the shots ain't great but it's nothing he ain't felt before. He looks at the bedside clock. Nine. Ah fuck. Checkout's eleven and he's already awake, coulda slept longer. Instead he puts on the crap coffee machine halfway between the bed and the bath-room, walks to the toilet and pisses awhile, gets in the shower like he'll never leave. But it ain't that good a hotel, the hot water fades fast and he gets out and kind of dries himself and walks out of the bathroom and onto the carpet still dripping, pours himself a coffee into a Styrofoam cup and drinks like it's good.

His main problem is he's doing nothing on the job until he hears back from Juke so this morning was supposed to be about talking to Carla. Not that it figured to be easy, but she has to know how much he expects to make on this job so she can see he's taking care of her and Malik.

Everything can be fine now, the three of them can be back together. Better than before. He remembers before, knows that ain't what she wants. But he don't have a clue what she does want.

He walks back and forth between the shower and the bed, towels off and drinks bad coffee. Feels like shit but that's the day he's given himself. No sense feeling that here and paying for another night. He checks out at ten to eleven, takes a cab to where his car's parked. Thank God he remembers that.

Nowhere to go right now, which he guesses means home. Taking Rommel out won't require energy; the dog runs on its own, not with him. Good. If Tommy moves fast in any direction he's gonna puke. Maybe drive Rommel somewhere. Fuck Carla and Malik, he knows his dog loves him.

He drives to the house and parks but he thinks of Carla all the way and damned if he knows why he's here. Opens the front door and Rommel greets him, excited. Earlier than Malik walks him, earlier than anyone ever comes home. Tommy grabs shit bags and a bag of treats, clasps a leash onto Rommel and they go to Tommy's car. Tommy pats the back seat and Rommel leaps up, lies down.

They reach the off-leash area at Berkeley Marina and Tommy lets Rommel go, slaps him on the flank and Rommel runs. Tommy has one of those plastic grips that holds a tennis ball arm's length and he pulls it back behind his shoulder and throws. Rommel takes off to fetch. This can go on for hours. He's a smart dog and Malik has a more advanced routine with lots of tricks but Tommy don't know all that. He has the stick with the grip and he throws the ball and walks forward and Rommel runs for it and brings it back. They'll do this as long as Tommy can stand it, interactions along the way with whatever dogs they come across. Leave it to Rommel and they might never leave.

Tommy wings the ball and Rommel runs. Rommel loves running and Tommy loves seeing that. The pleasure of running and retrieving, a joy too simple for his life. Tommy's life is fucked because he needs more. Run and retrieve is basically his job, and he's good at it. The problem is how he's treated when he brings shit back. Carla knows he's good at what he does or he'd be dead, but she don't love him for being good at it. Whatever he brings back is the dead bird in the cat's mouth, what you don't want in the house. Until it becomes the guy who brings it that you don't want in. He shakes his head. He feels like shit but keeps throwing the ball. Not like he wants to drink coffee or eat, not like he has a home to go to and relax. All he has is time until he hears back from Juke, and time's a fucking blade that twists and keeps twisting.

It's beautiful by the water and if it was the weekend there'd be broads to look at but there ain't. There's just throwing the ball and walking forward a few steps before Rommel brings it back. The way his body feels, this is the best he's gonna do the next couple hours. A few tours around the park then he takes Rommel away, to that place called home because it's where he sleeps most nights.

He sits with a beer on the couch and waits. It ain't drinking, it's hair of the dog, he's becoming human for when she gets here. It's getting so he don't know where she stands. He wants her to stand *with* him. Rommel's beside him, that's all he can count on.

Sports highlights are on the TV but no games this early. He waits, he watches, he grabs another beer. There's a sound at the door, someone coming in. He didn't hear a car. He gets up, walks into the kitchen. "Hey, Malik."

The boy stands at the fridge, turns his head as he opens it. "Hey, Dad."

"How's your day?"

Malik grabs the carton of milk, leaves the fridge door open, walks to a cabinet and grabs a cup, fills it. "Okay."

The boy drinks then walks the carton back to the fridge, shuts the door.

"Anything new?"

Malik shakes his head.

Tommy shrugs. "So, you learned nothing, talked to no one..."

Malik smiles. Looks charming, he's a good-looking kid. "Nah, but that's every day. You said new."

"So you learned something?"

"Algebra. Always learn something there."

Tommy shakes his head. "What a waste. That's nothing for us to talk about."

Malik laughs. Tommy don't know shit about math, but he and Carla have pushed Malik in it.

"So," Tommy says, "you talk to someone interesting? You got a girl?"

"Same guys I always talk to. Nothing special with a girl."

"Sounds boring. You sure you ain't my age?"

Malik grins, but this one looks more polite than

appreciative. Tommy's always had this problem with the boy, where he don't know what to ask to get a real answer. Carla has conversations with Malik. Tommy has interrogations.

Malik chugs his milk, walks out of the kitchen. Tommy follows as far as the living room, but Malik's down the hall to his room. Tommy returns to the couch and his beer. Returns to waiting for Carla, watches some sports talk show. Finds out Michael Jordan's hands were bigger than LeBron's, almost as big as Wilt's. And this Greek kid on the Bucks has bigger hands than that. Figures that's okay if you make enough money, but if you live somewhere cold and you gotta buy custom gloves? There's shops for big guys, but not like that.

His own wardrobe could use some work, but not because he has to custom order stuff. Just money's been tight so he ain't bought a shirt in years. They start looking old and who's gonna wanna work with him? Ragtag guys on the way down, has-beens and never-beens. So, all right, after this job he'll buy a few shirts. He hates stores, though. A bunch of straight assholes standing around. Maybe he'll buy some off the back of a truck.

He drinks, he waits. No matter how sober he is, Carla gets home and sees he's had a couple beers and it's gonna be The Showdown. Not the first and better not be the last, but she's gonna call what he's done drinking, not gonna notice or care that he's just winding down. She attacks and if he attacks back it's over, she's silent and walks away or stands there and makes him wish she'd walk away. Or he tries to explain and she attacks more. There's no way to win, she plays by women's rules. The way she acts when they argue, he wonders how she ever liked him, or if she never did and has just been on some reforming crusade this whole time. And he knows he's fucked because no matter how far gone she is, he wants her. And she's coming home soon and he don't know if that's what she wants at all.

Now the talk on TV has moved to more pressing subjects, which teams and players are hottest as the NFL playoffs approach. But it's like everything else; when they talk about players they focus on the ones who play the "skill" positions, quarterbacks and receivers and running backs, the guys who make the pretty plays, and barely mention the big men in the trenches who beat the shit out of each other all game and make all those pretty plays possible. There's guys who do the dirty work and the guys who let them do it and make the big money behind them.

Tommy don't like that thought, don't like much of anything as he hears Carla pull into the driveway. But it's not like the taste on his lips, in his mouth, is some smoky whiskey. Only a couple beers, nothing to change a man.

She's coming in and he's looking casual, relaxed, not straightening on the couch. He hears the door open and tips his head back, raises his voice. "Hey, hon'."

No holler back, just footsteps. After a minute she steps into the living room. "Hey, Tommy."

Not really a greeting, just she knows he's here, sees he's drinking and watching sports and steps behind the couch toward the hall.

"How's your day?" he says.

"Okay." She keeps walking.

Tommy's off the couch and behind her. "What the fuck? You just ignore me now?"

She looks back, turns and faces him. "Give me a reason not to, Tommy."

"I'm your husband. I love you. I know we got problems but I told ya, I got shit goin' on gets 'em took care of."

Her eyebrows go up. "You're gonna solve the money problem. Then everything's good. That what you think?"

"It's a step. I know it ain't everything."

"It's nothing. Pay attention. Stop drinking. Talk to us."

Tommy shakes his head. He don't know what his body might do, holds it back. He loves her. "You're wrong. It's a start. You're used to the other shit and I'm done with that."

"You're not listening." She turns and walks away.

He watches her walk to the hall. God she pisses him off. And he wants to fuck her, what a goddamn walk. She turns the corner and he goes back to his beer, stands and drinks. The TV's just a sound and a picture, nothing he takes in. He finishes the beer and follows the path Carla just walked, into the hall and down to their bedroom.

He opens the door.

Her bare back to him, she stands at the dresser, a drawer open in front of her. "You gonna shut that door?" she says without looking back. "Or you want Malik to see this?"

He shuts the door. "I want to see. Look at me."

She takes a T-shirt from the drawer. "Fuck off, Tommy." She pulls it over her head.

He steps fast toward her.

Dressed, she turns. "What the fuck you gonna do? Rape me? That how you love me now?"

Tommy shakes his head hard. "I never touch you like that."

"But you want to. Fuck off, Tommy."

His hand comes up and swings but she steps back and so does he. Knows if he hits her everything's dead forever.

"Get out."

She says it and he turns, walks away.

CHAPTER EIGHT

Tommy wakes alone in bed. Carla and Malik have already left the house. His head throbs but it's a two-ibuprofen hangover; he washes them down with a slug of water while he makes coffee. She don't get how much he loves her but he'll make her get it. That's not what today's about. Juke's gonna call this afternoon. The Manatee has to go down or Carelli fucks him up. When Juke tells him if Joey's in on the pickups, he knows what to tell Dunbar.

The water boils and he pours his coffee, looks in the mirror over the sink. He looks like shit. Not the first time. Turns with his cup and sips. Rommel watches. The microwave clock says eleven. Enough time for a short walk. Tommy smiles at the pit bull. Only one in the family he's sure loves him.

He takes his coffee to the living room couch, sets it on the table and picks up the remote. Rommel jumps up beside him. Tommy pets the dog's head, turns on the TV. ESPN in the morning—NFL Live. Good, something he can watch. It's late enough in the season the only good subject is projecting playoff teams and how far they might go. A few teams with a chance to go deep and the rest are losers. Exactly how the world plays out, and when he gets this Manatee thing done, he'll be one of the winners.

He finishes his coffee fast, crosses the room to where the leash and shit bags are. Rommel follows, sits at attention until his leash is attached, then guides Tommy to the front door.

They're back an hour later. Tommy taps the remote on his way to the kitchen, starts more water for coffee and opens the fridge, grabs the bacon and eggs, sets them on the counter. He cooks the eggs slow but the bacon's ready almost as fast as the coffee. He walks with his cup and a strip of bacon into the living room, turns up the volume so he can hear the football talk from across the house, and returns to watch his eggs. Everything right now is fuel. His hangover no longer hurts but he's numbed himself to get this far and he needs to be sharp.

Breakfast done, he waits. Like he's paying attention to the football talk, he sits on the couch and pets Rommel. He runs through his head what he says to Dunbar if Joey knows about The Manatee. He wants Dunbar on the job and maybe he talks him into crossing Smallwood.

Mid-afternoon and Tommy's had sandwiches and the TV's talking basketball pregame when Juke finally calls. "Good news."

"We meet at a different place," Tommy says. "You ready?"

"Yeah, what's the place?"

He names the one he dragged Amanda out of, gives the address. "And, Juke? Your nice clothes won't fit in there."

"I look good wherever I go."

* * *

Tommy gets a beer and a small table. It's the only size they have. Tommy committed assault in here a few days ago but he's gotta test whether he can just walk in. Watches the bartender, same guy worked the other night. He don't tell Tommy to leave, just serves guys drinks like he's paid not to remember. Good policy, a joint like this. Ban people for fighting, you might lose all your regulars.

Juke walks in a few minutes later in his usual nice suit, nods at Tommy, catches some looks and clearly don't give a fuck, gets a beer at the bar and sits at Tommy's table.

It's early. The place ain't crowded yet, no one sits near them.

"Fang's gone cowboy on this. Too far in to ever let Joey know." Juke removes a slip of paper from a jacket pocket, slides it across the table. A phone number. "That's Dunbar."

"So this guy Fang, he thinks he takes a piece and Joey never hears about it?"

"Don't know what Fang thinks, how he thinks, if he thinks."

Tommy looks at Dunbar's number, makes sure he can read it, pulls out his wallet and puts it inside. "You know that time we was in there?"

Juke nods.

"Notice protection at the tables?"

"Sittin' there?" Juke shakes his head. "Nah."

"Cuz there wasn't. Maybe on a Saturday. We went on a Friday, remember?"

"Yeah, sure, I had plans later."

Tommy drinks. "You always got plans later. Thing

is, Friday night? We could take this place inside. Take out the muscle in back. Do it quiet, no back door to go out. Gotta walk out front with the money."

"Take 'em out?"

"Not permanent. Tie 'em up, shut 'em up."

Juke don't nod, don't say anything, but he gets it. Tommy sees it in his eyes.

"We don't get the Saturday money," Juke says. "But we get away."

Tommy grins. "Alive."

Juke nods.

"So you'll do the job."

"I'd never cross you, Tommy. I know the payback. The job, sure. But you go to Joey after, about Fang? I get a piece of that too."

"You fucking crazy? I tell him that, he takes The Manatee money."

Juke shakes his head. "You think The Manatee's about the money? Joey gonna find out. It's about Joey. We get in good with Joey, we set."

"Gotta think about that. Might be complications."

Same bar, a few hours later. Tommy's gone to dinner and come back. Now he waits.

Dunbar walks in. Second guy today wearing a suit in here, although his is nowhere near as nice as Juke's. Probably the only guys to wear suits here in years. He sits. Even doing that he's clearly taller than Tommy. Tommy's wider, gotta make sure Dunbar knows who's in charge.

"No table service," Tommy says. "Get yourself a beer. And a Lagunitas for me." He drinks from his glass.

Dunbar walks to the bar. His suit's rumpled, like he's been awake too long. Or maybe that's just how he wears a suit. He comes back with two glasses, sets one in front of Tommy and sits.

"Why just you and me?"

Tommy breaks down the changes, how they don't need Smallwood for the job no more and it's better to pull the job on Friday and there's a guy works for Joey Lee involved only Joey definitely don't know about this.

"Ah, fuck." Dunbar drinks. "You sure Joey don't know?"

"Got it from Carelli. My guy says the same. Joey finds out after the robbery and we ain't killed his man, he goes after the guys who run the joint. Not us."

Dunbar nods. "So what's your plan?"

"On a Friday three of us with guns can walk out with the money, no shots fired. Unless someone inside gets stupid." He shrugs. "We got a driver with a gun outside, just in case. Anyone shows up ain't suppose to, he lets us know, we deal with it. And we drive away with a decent chunk of what we'd get on Saturday, but with a lot less chance of gettin' killed."

"You sayin' we make more on Friday 'cause we split it less ways?"

Tommy shakes his head. "We get more cuz we don't die."

"Why you think Smallwood don't go for that?"

"Ever work with Smallwood on a job like this?"

"Smaller stuff," Dunbar shrugs, "but he knows what he's doin'."

Tommy shakes his head. "Guy's strictly small time, gonna get someone killed. You want dead, or you want money?"

Dunbar nods. "But it's a four-man job, and you don't like Smallwood—he one of the four?"

Tommy picks up his glass. "Maybe he goes away. Thing is this: I gotta trust my driver. I already got that guy. And I gotta trust both guys who go inside with me. That's you and one other. I'll get the other, I'll know I can trust him. How do I know I can trust *you*?"

"You don't trust me yet, why you want me on the job?"

"One way I trust you. One way you work this job."

"Smallwood?"

Tommy nods. "And the body gets found. I don't take no one's word for nothin'."

Both men take long drinks.

Tommy stays at the table, sips. The way Dunbar answered the shit Tommy said, he ain't worked any big jobs. That's why he listens to Smallwood, why Tommy never heard his name before.

Juke waits outside. When Dunbar leaves, he'll follow. A chance Dunbar's dumb enough to go to Smallwood. Or maybe he goes to The Manatee, checks it out himself. Not a lot of point in that, no one said nothing about pulling the job on a Wednesday. Any restaurant's busier Friday and Saturday nights than weekdays. Difference at The Manatee is how much muscle's in there on a Saturday. Friday night might get crowded, but Tommy don't give a fuck how many people are there eating dinner. Those folks reach for anything it's likely a fork.

Tommy drinks, waits for Juke to call but he finishes his beer and there's one seat at the bar and he don't need a table no more. He takes the open stool, has his next beer there. The guy on his left talks to someone on his left and the guy on his right talks to someone on his right. Getting ignored in a crowd, feels just like home. Tommy orders another beer and a shot, waits for his drinks. There's a tap on his shoulder.

He ducks and turns, hand inside his coat.

"Hey," she says. "We're both a few days early, but no need to panic. Still might be a good thing."

Amanda. Looking good as last time, only a lot more sober. Him, he figures, not so much.

He stands, shoves his stool toward her. "Only seat at the bar." He looks behind her but the crowd's rolled in by now, all the tables full. "I can stand."

She pulls the stool forward, sits. He turns sideways to look at her, leans on the bar with one elbow. His leg's against her bar stool. He's up against the guy on his right. He looks that way and the guy's looking at him. Tommy glares and holds it and the guy keeps his mouth shut.

Tommy turns back to Amanda. "You still drinkin' Tequila Sunrise?"

She shakes her head. "I'm past that tonight. You think you know bourbon?"

"Ain't what I'm drinkin', but yeah."

"Impress me."

Tommy waves at the bartender, finishes his beer. The wet-haired guy behind the bar comes over. "Knob Creek. Two glasses."

Amanda smiles at Tommy. "You finished your beer. Now we gotta talk between drinks."

"We don't. But I got no problem if we do."

"You playin' tough?"

"Lettin' you know I don't talk a lot, that's all. Maybe you don't need to know. But this goes a ways, don't tell me I ain't talkin'. Sometimes I ain't."

"So you think we might last and you don't want us to? Fine. We're still here. Ain't gotta go past this."

Tommy's standing, his right hand leaning on the bar. He grabs hers with his left. "Said I don't talk much. Ever. Got better things to do."

She pulls away from him. He lets go of her hand. "You think I'm yours cuz we run into each other twice in a week?"

The bartender approaches with their drinks.

Tommy grabs her hand again. "That ain't why." He leans in to grab his glass. She takes hers and their bodies brush against each other. Both are leaning forward as they drain their glasses. No words as they walk out hand in hand.

Amanda wants bourbon. Tommy figures a pint is enough, gets a fifth. He kisses her in the car and she leans into him quickly, pulls back. "Let's go."

He drives to a motel that'll do just fine. Cheap but not the cheapest. Being with a guy on the edge has to be part of the thrill for her; spending money on a nice place would cheat her out of that. And it's a waste of money if they're just drinking and fucking.

She flips on the light as she enters the room, sets her purse on the floor and sits on the edge of the bed. He locks the door behind him, crosses to the chintzy desk with the TV on it, sets the bottle there, eases out of his leather jacket and hangs it on the room's lone chair.

"Oh," she says. She's turned her head enough to see his shoulder holster, .38 inside. Good, she's looking at him. He takes off the holster and drapes it over the coat.

"Get two cups from the bathroom." They won't need cups, he just wants her to do what he says.

She gets up, a look in her eyes the gun must've put there, walks to the bathroom like she's had as much to drink as he has, comes back with two paper cups, stops several feet from where he sits.

He cuts into the bottle's black plastic seal with a large knife, peels back enough plastic to open the fifth, takes a slug, and holds it out to her.

She drops the cups on the floor, steps forward until the bottle's in reach, takes it, drinks. "Same stuff?"

"Read the fuckin' label."

She doesn't bother, takes another drink and passes the bottle back to Tommy. "Why do you carry a gun?"

"Ain't suppose to. Ain't gonna get shot."

He won't confess to any crimes, and he *will* get laid. Perfect date.

She sits where she was before. He stands over her.

It's been so long, and god it was good. They lie there and he knows, like he's known every time, his marriage is dead and he's the one killing it. But that can't be what it is, he loves Carla. She's his goddamn life, she's just not seeing it right now. They get a couple things sorted, all this goes away. But right now he needs this, she's pushed him to it. No way he fucks around if he's getting fucked at home.

He wants the bottle and it's on her side of the bed. Amanda lies on her back so he rolls on top, kisses her, rolls back, grabs her by the chin and kisses her again, lets go. "Gimme the bottle."

"You were right there." She raises her eyebrows but

104

he just looks at her and she grabs the bottle. He turns so his dick's against her ass, cups a tit with one hand and she sits up so he can cup the other, then he's getting hard again and she lies face down and raises her ass. It's beautiful and he licks it then he's inside her again and the fucking goes on awhile this time.

"Oh God." She lies beneath him and he's glad to be on top of her. He grips her shoulders, nips at the back of her neck, don't want a goddamn thing less than everything. He comes and collapses on her, grabs the bottle from the table and rolls away.

She turns over and smiles. "So that thing about having a drink before. It was all a ploy?"

He's sitting up, holds the bottle by its neck, its lid off. He shrugs. "How I like to drink."

The smile stays. "I like drinkin' with you."

She kisses him and he kisses back and it's hot but no way anything else happens off this.

"Yeah, Amanda. Me too." He closes his eyes.

CHAPTER NINE

A different bar tonight, one Tommy's never been. He sits with Juke at a small table. It's afternoon and there's no table service; no one sits nearby. "I'm waiting to hear what Dunbar does."

"You told him to handle Smallwood? Or he's out?"

Tommy nods, drinks.

"So we need a fourth guy."

"And he's gotta be good. Say, that thing last month with Fat John. You know who handled it?"

Juke runs a finger around the lip of his glass. "Yeah. Karma took care of that."

Tommy looks at him funny. "What the fuck? You gone all hippie?"

"Karma D'Angelo. He just came home. You didn't know?"

"That crazy wop thinks he's Robin Hood?"

"Yeah, ya barely gotta pay the bastard. He thinks he's doing justice."

"All we ever do, man. All the other guys do too." Tommy shakes his head. "Won't fucking work. Can't trust a guy like that."

"There's a kind of guy you can trust?"

"Not a kind." Tommy takes a drink. "But there's a

guy. Look around anyway, in case my guy can't. I know who I want."

The news is no place to hear about an Oakland murder unless there's something special about it. And word hits the street slow when the victim's a nobody. You sure can't ask the question when you're involved in the hit. So Tommy stays in this place where no one knows him long after Juke leaves. But he's drinking beers slow in case Dunbar crossed him. He'd ask Carelli or Eddie what they know but those guys are impossible to get hold of at night, at least if you rank where Tommy does. They don't even know he's on his way up, think he's who he's always been. That all changes if he lives through this.

He drinks his beer slow, finishes and gets up. There's still no waitresses, never will be. He walks to the bar, orders another, returns to his table. He's halfway through the beer when his phone rings. Amanda. "Yeah."

"I just got to the bar and you're not here. You coming down?"

"Not there. Meet me here."

"And the name of the place?"

"Jacks or Better."

"I know it," she says. "I can be there in a half hour."

Funny, he thinks, looking around the near empty room. Don't look like no one knows it. "Okay."

The room's near empty and none of these assholes is worth a damn. Amanda might not be worth one either but he needs someone to fuck. She don't treat it like a favor neither. 'Course, she acts like she just needs a fling, and that's perfect if it's true. But he don't know shit about her, she just showed up, like Smallwood just showed up. He needs Eddie in on this so he don't feel like he's getting set up as the fall guy. For what, he don't even know. Eddie's a natural on muscle work, a perfect fourth guy for the job.

Tommy's on his next beer when Amanda walks in. He's glad to see her but he waits. Never run to a woman. Or from a man. One way or another he's gonna get fucked. Just one way's a whole lot nicer.

Tommy checks everyone on the street as he walks out with Amanda, but he always does that. The odds of being seen going from one place he's never been to another—he ain't being watched that close, no matter what. Not yet.

They get in her car. He didn't bring his, knew he wouldn't drive home. Or wherever he ended up.

"Where to?" she says.

"Turn left in a few blocks. Straight for now."

She drives, don't need to stop for something to drink this time. Tommy's buzzed, not hammered, should wake without a hangover. There's gonna be sex and it's gonna be great, then they sleep. When he wakes his problems at home will be worse because he didn't come home. His other problems? Same as now.

When this job's done he's in line for big money work. Just keep Joey Lee out and get Carelli his cut. Then plenty of work coming Tommy's way. All he has to do is stay alive.

Early evening, December so it's dark. Tommy's at Eddie's.

"Both?" Eddie says.

Tommy shakes his head. "Just a beer." Eddie brings

it over. "Hey, Eddie. One of those jobs you helped me get? Could use one more guy. Your kind of work."

"I like the work I got."

Tommy raises his glass. "You like the other kind, too."

Bar's crowded, plenty for Eddie to do. "Come back tomorrow. In the morning." He walks away.

Tommy finishes his beer. Eddie's working and it's Friday night. The Manatee's gonna get pulled on a Friday night. But Eddie don't work every shift and it's his bar. For what The Manatee should pay, he'll get the shift covered.

Tommy stops at a liquor store six blocks from home, the closest one that sells decent bourbon. Gets out his phone before he goes in, calls Dunbar.

"Hey," Dunbar says.

"Never mind hey. Is it done?"

"It makes the news if you look close enough. No one saw it happen but yeah."

"I go back to what I was doing then." Dunbar doesn't argue so he got out of the car, entered the store.

The Arab guy with receding silver hair sits behind the counter with his head down, asleep.

"Hey, boss," Tommy says, and the Arab looks up. "How ya doin'?"

"Tired."

"I can tell." He nods up at the highest shelf. "A pint of Maker's."

"A pint?" The Arab hesitates. Tommy always gets a fifth.

"Yeah."

The Arab turns, reaches, puts the bottle on the counter

where Tommy can't reach and rings him up. "Nineteen seventy-one."

Tommy has a twenty out, hands it over. The Arab hands him the bottle and Tommy puts it inside his jacket.

The Arab counts out the change.

"Someone needs that, give it to him." Tommy walks away from the coins and out the door, drives the last couple minutes home. He's had one beer, and he only has a pint as backup. He'd better get fucked tonight.

He walks through the empty kitchen. Expected someone to be there. Walks into the living room. No one there either. Fuck, she better not have left him. She wouldn't take Malik out of school. He repeats it to himself as he walks down the hall to the bedroom. Hears voices inside, opens the door.

She sits up fast, alone in bed with her laptop. That's where the voices come from. "What the fuck."

"I didn't see no one," Tommy says, knows he's just shown fear. "I had to find you."

"Jesus." Her head rolls back, returns to glare at him. "It's Friday night. I'm burnt out from work. Malik's a teenager, he's out with friends. God knows where you been. You gonna tell me about last night?"

"I was drunk," Tommy says. "Crashed at a motel."

"Right." She glares. "And every Friday night, this is normal. Only this time you show up at a reasonable hour. And don't know what to expect, cuz this is something you never do."

"I'm doing something different." Tommy's arms tremble at his sides, he don't know why, he ain't cold. "I'm getting out of this, getting to another level. And I worry about you. About you and Malik."

"You worry about *you*. You thought I left you, ain't that it? And maybe I will and that scares you. Glad it does but you gotta do something about it, Tommy."

"I'm gonna drink." Tommy shrugs. "That's who I am. You loved me like that before. Not when it got outta control, but I'm done with that. I don't drink as much and I make good money now. Getting better."

"And what do you talk about? You? Nothing Malik cares about. Nothing I care about."

The pint's inside his coat but he don't dare open it. "I ask about your day."

"You should know some of it by now. And what Malik cares about. You wanna hang on to any of your son, you need to show you care. You need to pay attention. Now."

Tommy shakes his head. "This ain't how I grew up. I talk about me, you talk about you, he talks about him—that's a conversation."

"It isn't." She sits up straight, adjusts the pillow behind her. "And you can't rely on what I felt when we met. I was a girl then."

Her black hair falling short of her bare shoulders, she still looks like a girl to him. He can't tell her, because he wants her that way and he knows right now it won't happen.

"You're older," he says. "You know about the world. You know this is what we are."

"We?" She cocks her head. "You mean us?"

"Nah." She don't get it. "Men. We drink, we like women, we do things our way."

"That's your world, Tommy. Not everyone lives there. Some of us care about other people. We find out about our children, what they care about, so when we ask questions, we get answers. You ask, 'How's your day?' and Malik says fine. What the hell is he supposed to say? He's fifteen and you're his dad and you can't ask a better question?"

"What's a better question than that?"

"Damn near anything. Find out what he cares about."

Tommy leans over her in bed. "How? What's he care about?"

She don't change expression. "Find out from him."

Tommy's all in motion now but he ain't going anywhere; his head and arms shake like they're undergoing electric shock; his heavy shoes stomp up and down.

Carla's out of bed, has him by both shoulders, but she's reaching up and he's much stronger than her, shakes her off as he continues with this thing that's maybe a convulsion and definitely scares the hell out of her. She grabs his shoulders and tries to hold him still but after a couple minutes, he's still shaking and she can't hold on, he's too twitchy. She should call 911, get paramedics, but all he does is shake and that's a thing he's done for years. It never escalates, not since he quit junk. He knows she'd be happier if doctors would take care of him but she doesn't trust any hospital with her husband, whatever he's become.

His shaking stops and she takes hold of his shoulders again, is about to let go when he falls backward and takes her with him.

Tommy wakes, alone and cold. Saturday morning, dim sunlight slips into the room. He wonders why he's cold; he's fully dressed. Including his jacket. Weird. On top of the blankets too. He rolls on one side and it's uncomfortable, he coughs and rolls back. Pats his inside coat pocket. A bottle. Oh yeah, he remembers buying the pint, but this makes even less sense now. How'd he pass out if he didn't drink?

He's half awake, some of this might be dreams, but he knows he yelled at Carla and that's when he passed out. But he's in *their* bed, the bed she's taken to calling hers. Maybe she stormed out after he yelled.

Back to the question then: what made him pass out? Stress, like these young guys always talk about? How worried could he be? There's always nerves before a job, but he's got this one about figured out. Is he still sick? Worse than he thought? Fuck, if it's that, the timing's terrible. The Manatee's everything.

Too soon to see Eddie, place ain't open yet. Until he does that, too soon to talk to Juke. But this whole thing where he's sick when shit's in the planning stages? Has to end. Now.

Tommy's up and in the kitchen, starts water for coffee. He walks into the living room, find out if Carla's ready for some. Couch empty, no blankets on it either. Nothing but Rommel, who looks at him like it's time for a walk.

"Little early for that, boy." Tommy walks down the hall but the bathroom door's open, no one inside. He walks on to Malik's room, knocks on the shut door. No answer. He turns the knob slow, peeks in, sees nothing, opens it wider. Malik's bed is empty, unmade but god knows from when. Likely the boy never made it home. Carla's probably coming back and the boy probably is too. No sure things.

Tommy goes back to the kitchen, pours his coffee. He'll make it through this morning, like maybe he's already made it through Carla and Malik. Or anyway, they'll be gone soon and he'll want them back but he won't have to figure them out anymore. Weird how other people live and think. Like their lives are the normal ones.

He leaves the kitchen, walks past Carla's little computer robot that plays her music and answers her questions, never his. He gives it a shot—"Hey Alexa, who gives a fuck?"—and walks out of the room, past its empty answer and into the living room, puts on some music on his old-school system, same stuff he's been listening to for years.

That always bugged her. "You still like the same music you liked when we met. Never anything new."

"What I like's good."

He still likes the same rock he always did, same as when she bitched because she asked him his sex fantasies and he just wanted to fuck, didn't need no damn fantasies. Now fucking Carla's a fantasy, and he wants everything about her but could settle for less, so long as less is good too.

After one coffee he wants another but Rommel keeps looking at him. Tommy looks back. When your marriage is fucked there's few things as sweet as making a pit bull happy. So he takes Rommel out for a neighborhood walk, a prelim to what Malik will give him this afternoon. Some of it's a run and Tommy needs the workout but he can't keep up the pace, has to call Rommel in with basic commands and treats to make him stop. Even with the stops Tommy sweats like a motherfucker, showers when they get back to the house, ready for more coffee and some breakfast and after that a meeting with Eddie.

* * *

He sees Eddie in the morning but Eddie won't talk business in his bar, sets it up for dinner at Chico's, a popular Mexican joint that don't take reservations. Tommy shows up early, asks for a table for two, gets called in after fifteen minutes. He's nursing a Negra Modelo when Eddie shows up.

Eddie sits, eats a few chips dipped deep in salsa. "Where's the fuckin' waitress?"

Tommy points behind him. "One of the young ones in a short skirt."

Eddie looks but they're all like that. He pats the menu in front of him with the palm of one hand. "Don't need this. Know what I want. What's the fuckin' job?"

It's crowded in here, too loud to understand the rumble of conversations at other tables but not so loud you have to yell your own. "A sports book. No one backs it. Gotta take it on a Friday night."

"What place? And why's it gotta be a Friday?"

"The Manatee. Near the lake. They mostly do the NFL, and they move the money somewhere else Saturday night. The move's protected heavy. The night before? Three of us can walk in and take it."

Eddie waves to a waitress across the room. "Why me?"

"You're good, I trust you. The other guy, he might need watching."

Eddie shakes his head. "Sounds stupid. Why use him?"

"He's a guy I have *now*. I gotta do this now."

"So, you're maybe puttin' me in a tight spot cuz you're in a tight spot."

The waitress reaches their table. A young, pretty Mexican girl. Dressed like that, she'll make plenty in tips. "Ready to order?"

"One a those." Eddie points at Tommy's Negra

Modelo. "And the beef fajitas."

"Steak ranchero for me," Tommy says, and they both watch as she scurries away.

Eddie turns to Tommy. "What's in it for me?"

"Your share's at least ten. And this—"

"I make ten and security's soft?"

"Maybe it's five, depends what they take in. But I been there. Security inside is weak."

Eddie taps the table a couple times. "And outside?"

"Nothin' on a Friday. And this guy you gotta watch, he's probably alright, and no way he crosses us during the job."

Eddie's head turns a little sideways. "You know he ain't with The Manatee people?"

"Not a chance," Tommy says, but it's a possibility he never thought of.

"You know him and you know them? You'd trust him if you knew him. Or wouldn't."

Tommy's lost, don't know what to say.

"You pay for dinner," Eddie says, "I keep my mouth shut. But I'm out. Deal with this guy you don't trust and you still need a guy, we talk again."

Tommy's mouth hangs open and he don't wanna sit there looking like that so he drinks. Who the fuck's he gonna get besides Eddie?

He sets his bottle down. "It ain't like that."

Eddie shakes his head, don't say a word. This conversation's over.

Tommy's still at Chico's, Eddie long gone. Tommy's at the bar, drunk but quiet, no one gives a fuck. What's he gonna do, who's he gonna use? He needs one more guy, gotta be someone extra good in case Dunbar has to be kept in line.

Tommy's past the Negra Modelos a while ago, except for washing down shots. His brain's a mess about all this but there's a Robin Hood guy, he remembers talking to Juke about him. Karma D'Angelo, oh god. Weird motherfucker, works on the cheap if he thinks it's for a cause. Tommy holds his glass halfway to his mouth, shakes his head. What's a fuckin' cause? What does Karma care about? And where can he find him?

The drinks here cost too much and the girls are way too young. It's a good goddamn thing he thought of Karma. He drinks, wonders who has Karma's number. Maybe the guy who told him Karma handled that guy.

He gets out his phone. He's too drunk to talk to a stranger about a job, and it's late but Juke's no stranger and he's not only still up but probably busy. Tommy calls, it rolls straight to message, he asks for Karma's number, ends it "Call me noon tomorrow," goes back to drinking shots. He'll get a cab somewhere, wake up somewhere. The rest of tonight don't mean a goddamn thing.

His head in the morning is ugly. Lucky him he can't see it. Motherfucker just hurts. He looks at his phone. Ten. Too goddamn early. And where the fuck is he, does he have to leave soon? Yeah, it's a bed and no way he's home, she woulda woke him hours ago. To bitch about something. So he probably has to be out of here in the next hour. He stays in bed, sets an alarm on his phone for ten-forty-five, closes his eyes. Fuck this.

When he wakes he goes home, loads up on ibuprofen

and lies down again, don't need to look good. Like he could.

He's half out when his phone rings and wakes him. He rolls over, grabs it and growls. "Yeah?"

"You wanted a number."

Juke.

"Sorry. Yeah. Fuck."

Juke gives it to him.

"He takes this," Tommy says, "he's the last guy, we go soon."

"Good."

They both hang up.

"Where witall, you know what that is? Means you stick it out, no matter what. Where witall. It's how a man lives after someone takes his reason. Like a gutted fish that ain't gonna die."

"Yeah, sure." Both men are sober, but damned if Tommy can remember what he asked that led Karma to that. He figures Karma's just one of those guys, talks about what he wants no matter what the question is.

Karma's a big guy with slicked back hair and a suit jacket like something could hide his gut. Not the jolly fat man either, too damn righteous. Sees weak people and thinks they need help. Most guys Tommy knows see them as prey.

He looks at the big man, don't know how to play this. "I got a job I think you'd be good at, Karma. But I gotta make sure we want the same thing."

Karma tilts his round head. "You mean money?" His face expressionless.

"I mean," Tommy says, "what kind of man you hate?"

"Hate?" Karma straightens up, shows teeth so white he must have paid for them. "I hate guys gotta hurt the poor to make money. Guys who can't just work for it."

"Good," Tommy says. "Cuz that's who we're dealing with. Guys who built their fortunes breaking people from their own neighborhoods. Now, the place we're taking down, they just fleece gamblers. But how do you think they built it?"

Karma nods, mouth tight a moment then open again. "Motherfuckers. What's the place?"

"The Manatee. Restaurant near the lake, sports book in back. They ship the money out under heavy guard Saturday night for football payoffs God knows where. Fridays? Almost all the money's there and four men can take it. Three of us so far. Sound good?"

Karma nods again. "Tell me more."

CHAPTER TEN

Rommel greets him at the house. Good, someone's happy to see him and no one else is here. His wife and son don't like him. He won't think of them by their names right now. He don't know who they are.

Tommy puts his new fifth in a cabinet, his six-pack in the fridge except one bottle he sticks in an inside jacket pocket, sticks a shit bag and a treat bag in two other pockets, puts the leash on Rommel's collar and takes him out.

They run. Tommy needs it but has no stamina, won't go more than a couple blocks. Rommel could run all day. It's Sunday afternoon and nice enough but it ain't spring, the sidewalks ain't crowded. Anyone in sight's gonna be an excuse for Tommy to slow it down to a walk. Their house is at the bottom of a hill and they run up the first block, turn onto a level street and still no one in front of them. A stop sign at the end of the flat block and it's a two-way stop and Tommy, breathing heavy, reins in Rommel at the sign. No cars and they cross but it's a fast walk, not a run.

Next block Tommy holds the leash tight and Rommel, well-trained, continues to walk, stops some places to sniff. This is the part of the walk where Tommy catches his breath. After a minute he's longing for Rommel to stop sniffing every few feet but the damn dog obeys its nose, not its owner. Malik's the one who trained him.

Two massive dogs off-leash on the next block, mastiffs or something. Rommel can handle them if anything comes up. Tommy keeps heading that direction, stops a second outside an apartment complex that's several feet above street level with a cement retaining wall three feet high. Tommy pulls the beer from his jacket, angles it along the top of the wall and bangs the cap off. He drinks and they walk toward the mastiffs.

Halfway down the block the black mastiff turns to them, alert. Each mastiff stands three feet tall and weighs at least one-fifty but the black one is wider, clearly the leader, stands a couple feet closer to them than the gray. Now the gray turns. Tommy takes a drink and he and Rommel keep walking. Rommel's not sniffing at the ground now. The mastiffs have their weight on their back feet, poised to attack. Tommy smiles. He likes dogs, but not all of them. Same as he feels about owners.

The black mastiff lets out with a thunderous bark: the King of the Jungle. Tommy don't care much for commands, takes another swig from his bottle and keeps walking.

Ten feet from the mastiffs Tommy sees something in the black one's eyes. He drops the leash and the black mastiff charges, the gray behind it. Tommy swings his bottle at the brick wall and it cracks in two, beer flooding out. He steps forward, the top of the bottle's jagged edges extended.

"Ferdinand! Come!" yells a bearded man from the back gate of a house just above the retaining wall. The black mastiff spins and leaps over the wall, through the open gate and into the bearded man's backyard. Rommel looks about to leap the wall but stops, turns. The black is gone and the gray keeps charging. Tommy steps forward, swings his bottle and crashes its side against the back of the gray mastiff's head.

"Dawes!" yells the bearded man.

The gray leaps, stumbles over the wall, through the gate and into the yard. The gray joins him and the bearded man shuts both dogs behind the gate.

Tommy looks up at the man in the yard above him. "Watch your fuckin' dogs."

The gate slams shut and Tommy drops his broken bottle.

A beer on the living room couch, winding down from the confrontation with the dogs. He hit the mastiff knowing Rommel didn't need help, but Tommy never could resist a fight. Wishes he could have hit the bearded guy instead. Dogs only act like that if they're raised like that. Tommy owns a pit, he knows.

Rommel was raised to protect Malik, to never start the fight but to always be a dog. Tommy knew a lot of guys who owned pits. He paid for a trainer so Malik would always be protected, whoever else might have to die. That included Tommy and Carla; that's what parents do, protect their children regardless. Carla's taking that an extra step now, keeping Malik away from *him*. Like he's a kind of man she don't want Malik to be.

But a man hits bottom, he don't need to stay there. Convincing Carla he's changed will be tricky, especially if she keeps holding it against him every time he has a beer or two. There's been a couple recent all-nighters, harder to explain, but until things get sorted she just has to deal with it. Only she don't see it that way. She don't have faith.

Voices outside, Malik and Carla. The front door opens and laughter enters the house, accompanied by the smell of hot pizza. Tommy gets up to greet them in the hall. Malik has a hand on either side of the large box, steps quickly toward the kitchen.

"Hey, Malik."

"Hey, Dad." Malik hurries past him into the kitchen, sets the box on the table.

Tommy follows him in. "Hot?"

Malik grins and gives his hands a quick shake in the air. "Yeah."

Tommy turns his head, smiles at Carla behind him. "Hey, Carla."

"Tommy," she says, her mouth not totally grim.

"You guys get Cokes?"

Carla glances at the beer in his hand. Tommy goes on, "I mean it's pizza. We should split a two liter."

"Sure," Carla says, like she don't know what's going on.

"Go ahead and start, just save me some." Tommy catches Malik smiling at him as he sets his beer on the counter and heads toward the front door.

The corner store ain't their corner, but it's only two blocks, he'll be home again fast. Things can get back to where they're supposed to be. Malik wants a good dad, Carla wants the man she fell in love with. Those things are four blocks round trip for the first step. Other steps will take him farther, but everyone wants this to work out. Who don't like pizza and Coke?

* * *

He still had to sleep in the living room with Rommel because he drank a few beers, but he got a casual kiss goodnight from Carla and friendliness from Malik and that's improvement with both of them. Plus Rommel may have saved his life today, so it's okay to sleep on the floor below him. Under a blanket, not feeling like anyone hates him. And tomorrow the whole crew gets together for the first time.

Which is today, he realizes, as Carla rousts him at way too close to dawn. But he does what he should, what any man would: crawls into the bed that still smells of her and sleeps as much as he can.

When there's no sleep left, he gets up slow. He lumbers to the bathroom first, and when a night's beer piss is done he walks into the kitchen to make coffee. Better if he had a coffee whore. She wouldn't need to fuck or blow him so long as Carla did that, just have his coffee hot and poured by the time he got to the kitchen. That's all the riches he wants, a woman who loves him and someone who serves him coffee the moment he wakes. Don't need to be the same person.

They used to have a coffee maker he could program but the goddamn thing never got the coffee hot enough. He threw that thing in the street the second day they had it and if someone blew out a tire, that was on the coffee maker company. Tommy and Carla went back to making single cups.

He opens the fridge and pulls out an unopened package of bacon. Turns on the oven, gets his coffee ready and takes a gulp, pulls two flat pans from the drawer under the oven and fills them both with bacon. He'll be on another coffee by the time the bacon's ready. Then eat and take a shower and head down to Eddie's.

Eddie's not working but the booths at his place are empty early afternoon. Great place for a quiet talk. Meeting's at one, Tommy the first one there then Juke and Dunbar, each with a beer when Karma shows up and sits with them at a quarter after.

"You're late," Tommy says.

"It's a meetin'," Karma says. "Won't be late for the job."

"You late for the job," Juke says, voice low, "I kill you myself."

"Never been late on a job," Karma growls. He gets up.

Juke stands too.

"I'm at whatcha call a disadvantage here." Karma waves his hand over the table, indicates everyone's beers. "I get back, we start on even terms." He walks to the bar.

Dunbar looks at Tommy. "Not a great start."

Tommy shrugs. "Always starts like this. Something like this."

"A guy's late?"

"Or he has attitude, or maybe that night don't work for him after all. Some bullshit. Gotta know the guy's worth it is all."

"Is he?"

"I don't invite him if he ain't."

Dunbar nods.

Dunbar took out Smallwood for this chance, Tommy figures he thinks that's enough to make *him* worth it.

Karma comes back with his beer. Dunbar sits to Tommy's left, Juke to his right, Karma across from him.

"So," Tommy says. He looks at Dunbar then Karma. "I hear you guys do good work. That's why you're on my crew. But when we go in, we go in heavy. Just the three of us. And I never worked with you before."

Tommy takes a drink, lets them weigh the words.

Dunbar answers first. "You sayin' you still don't trust me."

"I'm sayin' Juke's in the car and he got my back. Play this right, he got all our backs. And we split a pretty good haul."

"Whatta we do to get it?" Karma asks. "I don't give a fuck you trust me. Yes, no, don't matter. How's The Manatee run, what I gotta know. How we take the place and when."

"Goddamn soon is when," Tommy says. "How ain't tricky. Just gotta do it right."

Strip mall between Eddie's and home, Tommy stops for a couple slices of pizza and a tall coffee to sober up, gets a pound of mixed chocolates at See's and a vase of flowers from a corner stand. It's late afternoon but no one else is home yet besides Rommel, who don't bark when Tommy walks up to the door. He barks every time when the person approaching ain't family.

Carla's car ain't outside and Malik never comes straight home after school so Tommy don't call anyone's name, just sets the vase in the middle of the kitchen table with the chocolates in front of it, grabs the leash and bags and takes Rommel out. They walk a brisk couple blocks but Tommy feels tight, needs more exercise. He breaks into a jog and Rommel lopes beside him, obedient.

The sidewalks are empty in front of them. No need to

say anything to anyone, just move. Rommel the perfect companion, except they both want more. Rommel wants to run harder and do whatever else Malik has taught him. Tommy wants to fuck Carla and if it ain't her he needs someone else. He could go this many minutes fucking no problem. Jogging, there's no pretty motive in front of him. He slows to a walk a few blocks from a school with a grass field and leads them in that direction. Rommel can run off-leash there; he deserves it. Tommy will get what he deserves later. He just don't know where yet.

A dozen other people with half that many dogs in the grass field. The dogs run after thrown balls or play with each other or both. Tommy unleashes Rommel. Rommel sits, observing the action. A moment before Tommy realizes he waits for a command.

"Go."

Rommel runs, at full speed within a few strides. Tommy watches the other dog owners in this peaceful little play area straighten, alert at a level they rarely need to be here. And need to be now only long enough to watch the large pit bull sprint beside a decent-sized lab playing with smaller dogs and nip at it. They're the two largest dogs on the grass and they run off together, playfully nipping as they run until they're fifty feet from the smaller dogs. Then they're on each other, and a few people run toward them, two of them yelling.

Tommy walks slow toward the dogs. He smiles. This is play, and he knows it. Otherwise the lab would be dead by now, but they play rough together and they do it well, both holding back. From a distance that might be hard to tell but dogs are like anyone who likes to fight; something that feels like pain to others feels like life to them. It's how dogs need to play. Tommy knows it all too well.

They jog back the last several blocks to the house. Sweating when he walks in the no longer locked front door, Tommy doubts what he'd just been thinking: that he's in better shape than he thought.

"Hey!" Carla calls from the kitchen.

He hears her walking toward him, unleashes Rommel, and waits. He feels too gross to see her but always wants to.

She stops in front of him. "What's with the chocolate and flowers?"

She kisses him.

His arms go around her quick. "What you deserve." He lets go. "I need a shower."

"Come in, say hi to Malik first. He doesn't care you're dirty. You're his dad."

She leads and Tommy follows. He doubts Malik cares if he's there or not but she's being nice. And if she's right, it's something he wants too. It's just wrong when your kid don't like you.

Malik's at the kitchen table with a plate full of tacos plus one that he's eating.

"Hey, Malik."

Malik nods, his mouth full.

"There's plenty," Carla says. "Help yourself."

"Maybe later," Tommy says. "Leave everything out, I'll clean up. Right now, I gotta shower."

The last of Malik's taco enters his mouth.

Tommy tries him again. "How's your day?"

Malik shrugs, grabs a taco from his plate.

Tommy don't sigh or speak: no surprise here. He looks at the boy, who don't look up, just eats. Tommy looks at Carla and walks out of the room.

The shower's a good place to think. Tommy leaves it fuming. He takes his time toweling dry, puts lotion on his face—Carla says he needs it for his dry skin—and changes into sweatpants and a Justin Smith jersey, number ninety-four. He steps into the hall, dirty clothes under his arm.

Carla pushes herself off the wall she's been leaning against.

"You need the bathroom?" he says. "Coulda come in."

She shakes her head, steps up to him, talks soft. "Not a good night to talk to Malik. Keep doing this, stuff for us, and coming home sober and staying that way. He'll talk. But he's a teenager, you know. Falls in ruts and thinks he'll never get out. Gotta convince him you changed. Convince me too." She kisses him. Second time tonight. "It'll be nice."

Tommy's arms around her tight now, his face against her cheek. Hanging on to her tight as he can, not kissing back. Her arms come around him and it's what he was waiting for. She's holding him up. He didn't know he was about to fall. More like he was floating. Hell, maybe she's holding him down. Maybe that's what he needed and didn't even know. Still don't know, just holds her tighter and she holds him.

* * *

129

He's sitting up in bed when she finishes her shower and steps into the bedroom. The beers he had at the meeting would be enough for her to ban him from here tonight, but she don't know about those, and he hasn't had a drink since he got home.

She wears a long T-shirt that hangs lower than whatever else she's wearing, shows her off from the upper thighs down. Everything she shows looks great.

She turns out the light and slides in beside him under the blanket. "You know," she says, "it was good what you did tonight. And last night. Malik needs a dad who's here for us. Gotta do it more than one or two nights is all."

Tommy turns on his side, toward her. "I don't know what to say to him. He never answers."

"You gotta know what he cares about so you ask better questions. What's anyone gonna say if you ask, 'how's your day?'"

"Only he don't say what he cares about."

"I find out."

Tommy's eyes have adjusted to the dark now and he sees judgment in her eyes. Mostly though he sees her beautiful face near his and he puts his hands on her cheeks and kisses her. She kisses back, then his arms are inside her shirt and she sits up, raises her arms. They get her shirt off and his mouth is on one nipple then the other and she's on her back. Their bodies know and crave each other and they're going for it all tonight. And they'll get it, but it won't be a lifetime supply. Leaving something to look forward to tomorrow night.

He wakes up, she's gone. Four nights in a row now he's

slept with Carla, and he's been sober. The Manatee's tonight so no way he's been dealing with the stress without drinking, but it's always in the afternoon, no more than a beer and a shot each day. No less either, but he has fucking Carla to look forward to every night. That helps with the stress.

Late afternoon he writes Carla a note, says he's going out, don't say doing what. She'll know what. He sticks the note on the fridge. The job's not for a few hours but he can't just sit here and wait. Time to get with Juke. Coffee and sandwiches at a place down the road.

Tommy gets there first, orders a sandwich and sits with his coffee at a table. He waits in his leather jacket and jeans, a T-shirt under the unbuttoned jacket.

Juke walks in looking dapper as fuck, in a suit coat with black shirt and slacks that both look sharp enough to cut.

"You ever go anywhere dressed like someone normal?"

"The women I like don't settle for normal." He pulls out his chair.

"You and broads."

Juke sits.

"You wanna order anything, you gotta go to the counter. They bring food over, but you can't order here."

"Coulda said something before I sat."

"I was too worried I'm pulling a job with a sex addict."

Juke smiles and walks to the counter. Comes back, he's got coffee. Sits across from Tommy.

"So," Tommy says, "what you think of our partners?"

"Like, can you trust the muscle you're goin' in with?"

"Yeah, like that."

Juke sips from his cup, sets it back down. "Karma's good, he done this before. Don't know Dunbar. You

131

picked him."

Tommy nods. "He did a thing for me. Makes me think I can trust him."

"So, that it? You trust 'em both? We can pull this job now?"

"Last chance to call it off. We meet 'em in a couple hours."

"Weird you worry this close to the job," Juke says.

"Weird's the day I don't worry 'bout a job."

Juke double parks a block from The Manatee.

Tommy rides shotgun. "Be out front three minutes after we walk in."

Juke nods. They've been through this a half dozen times; Juke needed once.

Tommy gets out. Dunbar and Karma open the back doors and join him on the sidewalk. They're dressed well enough to go out for a late dinner and drinks, which is fine for The Manatee except they don't exactly look legit. But it's Friday night and they do look like the kind of guys who'd head straight for the sports book, which is what they do.

The three carry pistols under their heavy coats but that's second nature to them, and if the job makes them nervous they don't show it. Tommy sets the casual pace and the other two follow. It's late and Tommy has a bottle; they all had a shot before they came in. They might need the rest to calm down later. Or celebrate. Anyway, they'll drink it.

They get to the big guy outside the room in back. No one else around, Tommy reaches for the door.

The big guy holds out an arm like an iron bar in

front of Tommy's chest.

"We're here to bet some football," Dunbar says. He stands a foot to the big guy's right.

The big guy turns his head, considers Dunbar.

Tommy pushes down on the door handle and it opens. "Okay."

The big guy turns back to Tommy as Karma's .45 comes out. He swings and it catches the big guy under one ear, sends him sprawling to the floor. Dunbar's down there in a second with wire twist-ties. The big man's mouth is duct taped shut and his hands tied behind his back, his ankles tied together. There's an employee break room down the hall. No one takes a break there this late. Dunbar drags the big guy into it.

The room is near empty; they don't allow drinking back here, people just place bets and leave. Tommy and Karma join the short line to place bets. There's two guys in front of them but they look like no one to worry about. Dunbar returns with a set of keys from the big guy outside, quietly locks the door behind him. No more gambling tonight.

Three minutes or so for the first guy to place his bets, then it's the other guy's turn and the first guy walks toward the door. Where Dunbar stands, .38 in a hand hanging at his side, a dour smile on his face. He swings the pistol hard across the side of the guy's head. The guy drops, unconscious.

Karma yanks the guy in front of Tommy away from the window, slugs him with his pistol and the guy's out. Tommy's .38 is aimed between two rows of metal bars, at the cage teller's head.

"We get all the money in back," Tommy says, "or you're dead. Unlock that door." Tommy nods to his left.

Karma's heading in that direction. "Don't fuck with us. We're connected, you ain't."

The teller's eyes don't move when Tommy nods; they stay on the pistol aimed at his head. Tommy smiles. "My lucky pistol. No one lives when I shoot 'em with it."

Karma reaches the door.

"Now," Tommy says.

The door buzzes and Karma pushes it open, runs behind the teller, keeps his pistol aimed toward the back of the room.

"All you got here to me," Tommy says, "and what's in back to him."

The teller opens a drawer, fills a bag. It ain't much. "I buzz the back to come out, they gonna know something's up."

Tommy steps fast to his left. "Let me in that door too."

The teller lets him in and Karma heads to the back and Tommy grabs the teller. "Let 'em know now."

The teller presses another buzzer and Tommy wraps an arm around his neck and walks him ahead, trailing Karma. It's a big door back there but no way it's steel like a bank. Karma stands just outside where it'll open, Tommy and the teller a few feet behind. Karma's against the wall, his .45 pointed at the ceiling, gripped in both hands.

They wait. A phone rings up at the teller's stand. No one there to pick it up, it rings and rings. Another minute and the phone rings again. Over and over. Sick of their patience, Tommy pulls his pistol back and slams it against the side of the teller's head, knocks him bleeding unconscious to the floor. Tommy drops beside him, prone with his pistol aimed up at whoever might come through the door.

Another couple of minutes, no more calls. Karma stands ready to fire, Tommy lies the same.

The door pulls back slow. Karma stays back, Tommy stays down. Someone behind the door can get them the money. No way it's the first man they see.

Karma drops into a squat, curls into the doorway. A flash, deafening. Tommy sees the body fall and Karma clamber past him. Tommy stays low and follows. Fucking Karma don't give a fuck about murder one.

Everyone in back heard the shot of course. They're nowhere to be seen. Karma and Tommy duck behind a couch and slowly peer around either end; the idiots have furniture like it's a normal living room. Twenty feet beyond is a small bar with a back wall behind. No exits in sight, no people either. And not a fucking sound, but the guys with the money have to be back there.

"My name!" Karma shouts, no longer peering out, "is Karma D'Angelo! Throw out the money or you are fucked!"

Tommy waits with Karma, slumped on the floor behind a lousy couch. Of course no one throws out the money. It's been at least a minute.

Karma stands. Shots spray around him but he don't fall. His pistol comes up and he fires, turns, and fires again. No one fires in return. He steps out. After a moment, Tommy follows.

Tommy steps beside him. "What the fuck?"

"They missed," Karma says. "I didn't. Where's the fucking money?"

They step past a couple dead men. A safe in the wall. Tommy kneels. "This fucking thing? We got a payday. Just don't forget I got a guy out front."

"When there's gun shots? We get out how we can."

Ah, fuck. Tommy's good with safes but he gotta move fast. Because of Karma. "Gimme a minute. If I get this…"

"Ain't got a minute! We gotta blow!"

Karma's right. But they came for the money and now it's murder one and they ain't walkin' out empty-handed. It's a combination lock. Tommy puts his ear to it but he can't hear a thing, he just feels a churning in his stomach and ass. Jesus, great time for the sick to make a comeback.

"Let's go!" Karma yells.

"You're the one killed these motherfuckers." Tommy hears something, turns the dial slow the other way. If this thing's as discount as the rest of their security, it might only take a couple minutes. He constricts his ass so it don't burst. Something inside his gut's twisting up tighter than he can hold his ass. Like a strangler has a rope around his guts and the only way not to die is burst. Not as bad as when he was really sick, but still…Tommy hears another click inside the safe, turns the dial to the right again.

Karma's walking away. "Get it open fast then."

Oughta shoot the prick in the back, Tommy thinks. But I might need him. All that security they were trying to avoid is probably on its way now.

He turns the dial slow, hears another click, takes it back to the left. With luck this will be the last click and the money will be there. He thinks luck and he's focused on the lock and he can't hold back any longer. A dribble of shit runs out his ass and down the back of one leg. Normal sick, not like before, but dammit. He pauses from turning the dial to focus on holding this to a dribble, not a burst. He feels his insides clenching, feels the stare.

Karma. "The fuck is wrong?"

"It's nothin'."

"What's nothing? You been shot?"

"Forget about it." He pulls his hand back from the safe just before he shakes, woulda fucked the whole thing. The shaking stops and he gets his hand and ear back where they were. "We're almost done."

Karma turns around, walks back and opens the door that led them behind the teller, leans back enough to hold it open.

Tommy's got the dial turning again and more shit drips down his leg. He's trying to hold it but Jesus it hurts. He turns the dial slow. At last a click, louder than the ones before. He turns the latch below the dial and pulls the safe door open.

Stacks of money inside. "Karma!" Tommy pulls a bag from under his jacket and scoops an armload inside. Shit streams out of him and Karma runs to him.

"Jesus Christ!" Karma gets close. "Yer shittin'?"

"Get the money!"

Karma scoops and drops them in the bag. "Christ you stink!"

He empties out the safe while Tommy holds back more shit then they run through to the door guarded by Dunbar.

"What's that smell?" Dunbar yells. He opens the door and all three go through to the bar area. The plan is to walk casual but it's hard when one of your trio reeks of shit he's still spilling behind him. They walk fast, don't run, but all eyes are on them. No one's acting like security, though; they keep going.

They get to the front of the restaurant. Karma's been looking back all the way, that's his role here, but Tommy's the guy everyone looks at. He turns back too. A lot of wide eyes but no one makes a move.

Dunbar opens the front door. All three step outside. A gunshot and they drop.

Tommy is in the middle, Dunbar on his left and Karma on the right. Juke's black Dodge Demon is right in front of them where it's supposed to be. No sign of Juke. Opposite side of the street, to the right, is a Caddy sedan, one pistol out of each side window.

Karma is up first, on his knees and leaping left as the backseat shooter swings his pistol toward them. Tommy fires and rolls left, stops when he bumps Dunbar, who rolls. Tommy keeps rolling and a shot flies past him. Tommy looks back and another gunman's crouched at the back of the Caddy.

Karma rises from behind Juke's trunk and fires through the Caddy driver's open window, shoots him through his cheek. Tommy fires wild shots and he and Dunbar crawl behind Juke's car. Karma's already around the car and firing again. The backseat shooter disappears just as Tommy had him lined up. He adjusts to the rear gunman but stray rounds ping off the trunk and keep him pinned low. Next to him, Dunbar reaches over the hood and fires blind, not caring what or who he hits.

The rounds above his head keep Tommy prone, watching legs below cars. He sees Karma drop to a knee. A gunman comes around the front of the Caddy and Tommy fires at his legs. The way the guy falls to the ground Karma must have got him—he ain't moving after he lands—and no more pings on the trunk so Tommy stands.

But the backseat shooter's pistol is already out and aimed at Karma.

A shot, from Juke's car.

Another and the backseat shooter disappears once

more, this time with blood spattered on the back of his seat at what had been head level. Juke's pistol hand looms out his driver's side window. The pistol drops to the street and Juke falls back.

Tommy slogs around the car to his friend's door, shit falling from him all the way. Karma stands watch in case someone survived. Dunbar opens a back door. "We gotta go."

Karma opens the other back door but steps around it to Tommy, pockets Juke's pistol.

Tommy opens Juke's door. He's crumpled in the driver's seat, his right hand clamped on his left arm just below the shoulder, but if he's dying it ain't fast. "Move over," Tommy says.

Juke sits up and falls to his right, tries to pull himself to the passenger side, don't get far.

"Help me move him," Tommy says.

Karma starts to head around the front but Dunbar's already there, taking Juke by his unwounded arm. Dunbar yanks hard as Tommy pushes him over. In a minute Juke's enough out of the way and everyone's seated, Tommy behind the wheel. He lowers all the windows, hits the gas hard and Juke's head bangs off the passenger side door.

They get off the block and Tommy turns uphill, takes a turn going up then another, slows down. "Safer driving normal now. No one knows these fucking back roads behind the lake."

"Except you, I hope," Dunbar says.

"Me and the people who live here. No fucking GPS, that's for damn sure."

"Your buddy gonna die here?" Karma asks. "Or you gonna kill all of us with the smell of yer shit?"

The car levels off, no longer climbing hills, just goes from one street to another like negotiating a maze. "I ain't a doctor," Tommy says. "I think we can patch him up but I ain't even seen it. Gotta make distance first."

"I ain't dyin'," Juke says. "Just hurts like hell."

"Pass that bottle then," Karma says to Tommy and shakes his head. "You gonna wanna burn this fuckin' car."

Tommy pulls the bottle from his coat, hands it back to Karma.

"They get DNA from shit?" Karma asks, and takes a swig. Dunbar's hand is out and Karma passes the bottle.

"Fuck no," Tommy says. "That don't make sense. Anything I ate could be in there. Not who I am, just what's passed through."

"Yeah, well," Karma says, "spit. They get it from spit. And your spit's in your food, mixes in when you do that chewin'. And they get you, they gonna be lookin' where you been and who wit. You a sick motherfucker. I look that spit shit up and it's true? You a dead sick motherfucker."

Tommy guides the car from one street to the next. They're going downhill a little at a time, a gradual descent away from the lake. He looks back hard at Karma. "You know a guy got busted that way?"

"Never knew a guy shit through a fuckin' job."

"It don't happen." Tommy shakes his head, glances back quick but mostly keeps his eyes on the road. "They'd find piss in a toilet, bust a guy. Spit on a sidewalk, same thing. We're almost done with this job, then you never gotta know me again."

"Nah," Karma says, "you don't get off that easy. Ain't easy findin' guys work for a cause. Get well, motherfucker, or you get dead. You stay alive and fight for the people? Okay. You fuck this up for all of us? You goin' down. I got your back or I shoot you in it. Up to you how that goes."

The words in his head, Tommy drives. Karma is a problem. One more thing he gotta deal with. One way or the other. The other is better.

There's no talk, they get to the bottom of a mild slope and cut away from the lake.

Tommy comes down bearing left on 5th Avenue, takes the first right and drives up into numbered residential streets. No one follows no one here, too many dead-end streets.

"You got a guy patches shot guys?" Karma says. "Smellin' like shit's bad enough. You gon' give us a dead man too?"

"I ain't dyin'!" Juke says, but his head's tipped down, he's hard to hear with the windows open.

"He ain't dead or dyin' or even bleedin' far as I know," Tommy says. "Worry 'bout your own fuckin' self."

"Ain't how this works, you know? Murder's murder, cops don't fuckin' care who shot who. We was doin' the crime, so no matter who shoots Juke, we're up on it. You get that shit, right? Guy dies in the car I'm in and he got a bullet, I get blamed for the bullet. You too. And him." Karma nods at Dunbar. "Fuck, lotta murders in this city. Any stray they got they happy to stick on us. Evidence don't fuckin' matter once they say we're killers. You know that's how it goes, right? Keep your man alive."

"Juke ain't gonna die," Tommy says. "Only guys dead tonight is the ones you shot. So shut the fuck up about it." Tommy glares at Karma, returns his eyes to the road.

"Your man too."

"Savin' *your* life, asshole." Tommy drives a few minutes, pulls into a hotel parking lot. It's a decent looking place. He already has a room key. He gets out, nods at Juke as Karma and Dunbar open their doors. "He rests here. Only take a few minutes."

The three men go to the room. Tommy's the first one in but he waits inside the door, locks it behind them. All the money's thrown on the bed and each man counts it.

Dunbar's eyes widen. "Seventy-seven?"

"Minus what I charge," Tommy says. "Bringin' everybody in. You guys get a third of the rest."

"You swear Juke's gonna live," Dunbar says.

"He got shot in the fuckin' arm, motherfucker." Tommy clenches his fists.

"Sorry, shit, I forget he's your friend."

"You think I'd let him die and take his share?"

"Let up, pal," Karma says. "He's new at this, he's just lookin' out."

Tommy glares at Karma. "Shut the fuck up. I shoot both you assholes in a heartbeat."

"Or we divvy up the money," Dunbar says. "That's what we said, right?"

Tommy shakes his head at Dunbar. "Yeah," he sighs, "that's what I said. I'm taking thirty grand, my share plus finder's fee. You guys split the rest."

Tommy leaves out that the original finder is dead. Dunbar keeps his mouth shut and Tommy counts out thirty, sets aside another fifteen and change for Juke. Karma and Dunbar take theirs and Tommy drives them to their cars, throws the empty bourbon bottle into an alley as he drives past.

CHAPTER ELEVEN

Tommy walks away from The Manatee job thirty large to his name. He pays Carelli first thing tomorrow and he still has twenty-five to show Carla.

First, though, someone gotta take care of Juke, and Tommy's the only one gives a fuck. The shitty man takes the wounded man home. Tommy's home. Middle of the night but one good thing about a guy who gets shot like Juke did—he won't make a ton of noise, just a fucking groan once in a while. Depending on the guy, of course. More likely Carla wakes to Tommy's smell than Juke's groans.

It's late and Carla and Malik are in their beds. He can't put Juke on the couch, Rommel's there. And Juke has to lie down before Tommy can get in the shower. He don't even have a change of pants except in the bedroom and Carla's sleeping.

"I get you the couch," Tommy says, "take a chair for now." He guides Juke into the kitchen, sits him at the table, gets him a glass of water. He checks the fridge but of course there's no beers. Tommy never has leftovers.

Juke sits and Tommy goes to the bathroom. Cleans up best he can, wipes his pants with toilet paper but that's as good as he can get. He steps out. It's only midnight and

Juke should lie down a long time.

Tommy comes out to the living room, puts bags for dog shit in one pocket and treats in another and leashes Rommel. Rommel off the couch, he lays Juke down on it. It's the middle of the night and Rommel can probably run for eight hours or however long Juke needs to sleep. Tommy can't go that long even if he wasn't shitting. But he takes Rommel for their usual neighborhood walk, only he's still got his pistol on him, a gun he should have tossed by now. He'll get rid of it soon but for now it's protection. He still has the money too, his share *and* Juke's; figures it's safer to carry it than leave it at home.

They get back to the house and it's only been an hour and a half, too soon to wake Juke. They head out on the same route one more time. Not like he's got something to drink to help him wind down anyways. But after a double walk and shitting all the way he's gonna be desperate for that shower. And Juke can move to the floor. He'll split it with him after he's clean.

No sounds of violence from the houses and apartments they pass, loud talk and laughter is all. No cops and no one else on the sidewalks either, thank God. Tommy's carrying forty-six large, he ain't giving it up. And he better not have to shoot anyone; he don't feel like running afterward.

Rommel feels like running but he won't even try unless Tommy goes first, which ain't what happens. This time when they get back to the house it's three a.m. Tommy's done. Rommel stops at the couch, looks up at Juke lying there, growls soft then follows Tommy to the bathroom. Tommy walks in slow but shuts the door quick, keeping Rommel out, relieved he gets to drop soon. He holds his ass tight so he don't shit anymore as he walks to the toilet, hopes nothing falls from his pants.

Lucky break there, far as he notices. He sits on the toilet and more streams out. He sits awhile just in case, wants this to be over. When he finally stands he pulls his pants off, turns them inside out, and lets stray clumps of shit fall in the toilet before he flushes. He turns the pants back so he can wear them again if he has to, throws them across the room to the door, and gets in the shower. He stays a long time.

When he gets out he dries off, puts his shirt back on but wraps a towel around his waist, leaves his pants on the bathroom floor. The money's in his jacket so he puts that on too, joins Juke and Rommel in the living room. He grabs a couple spare blankets from the closet then takes Rommel's leash off. He rouses Juke, moves him to the floor and drops a blanket on him, walks a few more feet and pulls the other blanket over himself as he lies down.

Carla shakes him hard. Must be morning. She whispers, "Who the fuck is *that*? And the bathroom—" She shudders. "Both of you, out of here. Now. Before Malik gets up."

Tommy gets up from the floor, heads to the bedroom for clean clothes. Anyway, the pants he grabs are clean for now. Even when his ass ain't exploding it still leaks a little.

"And," she points toward the bathroom, "take those pants with you."

Tommy gets dressed, grabs the dirty pants from the bathroom and drapes them over one arm. He wakes Juke, helps him up, guides him out the door and into his car. Tommy still has the keys. He throws his filthy pants in the trunk, gets behind the wheel, and backs out of the driveway.

"I still got your money," Tommy says. "You remember that from last night? You okay?"

"Hurts like hell but it went straight through. And I ain't bleeding."

"You don't work out so much, you don't get shot at all. Fuckin' arm's too big."

"Someone oughta look at it." Juke's face is tight.

"Yeah," Tommy says, "and I know this part's my fault, but we gotta fumigate your car or somethin'. Those fuckin' pants in your trunk? First dumpster I see, I'm pullin' over."

"I know a guy. Take care of my arm, but he ain't cheap. The four of us should split it."

Tommy nods. "You and me split it for now, collect from the other guys later. Now, where's your doc?"

"Get on the 580 East."

He could've guessed that part. Most of the worst parts of Oakland are east of here. There's bad stretches to the west but they ain't near as big.

He drives a couple miles, gets on the freeway. "Did you see them?"

"Who?" Good, he's awake.

"The shooters, security. Was one Chinese?"

"Fuck if I know," Juke says. "You thinkin' Joey's guy?"

"If it's the same group picks up the money."

"Cops got the body by now."

"There wasn't time then." To grab it, Tommy means. Juke don't say nothing. He gets it. Ain't fucking complicated. Just fucking fucked up.

It's that idiot Karma opened fire and now it's murder one so he has to worry about cops 'til he's dead. And one of the dead guys maybe works for Joey Lee only Joey didn't know about this joint but he does by now. And God knows what Joey's gonna want but he's a mob boss. Usually, he wants everything.

Juke directs Tommy to the guy who's gonna patch him. A lot of these guys were good surgeons, just fucked up one operation. Too long a shift or drunk, don't fucking matter. Wrong man dies, someone gets punished, same in hospitals and on the street. It's all one world. One fucking bloody world.

Tommy pulls into the driveway, a nice house, nothing special. He helps Juke out of the car and to the front door, rings the bell.

A little guy in a Warriors T-shirt—the movie, not the team—opens the door, steps back to let them in. "What the fuck is this?" the little guy says, and nods at Tommy. "Shut the fuckin' door."

Tommy shuts it behind him. "About there." He points just below Juke's shoulder. "He said you take care of it."

The little guy looks Juke in the face. "I know him. You got money?"

"Yeah," Tommy says. "How much?"

"Ten."

Juke glares. "Motherfucker."

The little guy nods at Juke. "I'm sayin', ten's regular. But you steer a lot of traffic my way. For you, it's five."

"Five," Juke says.

"Best I can do. You wanna shop around, good luck."

Tommy's hand is in his coat.

"Bring the hand out empty," the little guy says. "You won't believe who's behind me."

Any worse than who's after me? Tommy thinks, but maybe Joey ain't after him. No sense adding to the men who want him dead.

Tommy's hand comes out. He flexes his fingers. "Had a itch."

"Full a shit," the little guy says. "See that bar over there?" He tips his head at one of those cheap kitchen setups you might see in your nicer mobile homes. They called 'em trailers when Tommy's grandparents lived in one. "Go."

Tommy takes a step over. Juke stands still.

"Both of you."

They walk to the bar, turn around.

"The way you were." The little guy don't show a weapon. "Lean on it like you been pulled over for somethin' brutal. Legs wide."

They turn, they spread. Tommy could warn the guy his hand might come up stinkin', but a guy makes him spread gets what he deserves.

He pats down Tommy first; Juke don't look dangerous and he's the one been shot. The little guy starts up top, finds Tommy's .38. "Fuckin' close to your itch."

No reason to answer that.

The guy keeps patting, goes between Tommy's thighs. "Christ, you get shot too? It's wet down here."

"Take a whiff, doc. That ain't blood."

"Scared, huh? But not shitless." One hand pressed hard against Tommy's calf so he still leans against the bar. The doc checks his ankles and stands, Tommy's Ruger in his pocket.

"Sorry, Juke, I'm not washing my hands before I pat you down. Just before I cut you open."

"You gotta cut me?"

148

He frisks Juke, shoulders to ankles, finds nothing. "You payin' me to ignore you? Gimme the money and go, I'm fine with it."

"Do what you gotta do, man."

"You wait here," he says to Tommy. "The front door's locked and I got the key. No slipping out to your car for another weapon."

"How long I gotta wait?"

The little guy shrugs. "You just gotta wait. But first I get paid."

Tommy counts out five thousand, hands it over, and the little guy counts it.

"Okay."

Tommy turns and sits on a stool as the little guy leads Juke to another room.

It's a couple hours. Tommy's raided the fridge and drank the two beers that were in there. He's moved on to a glass of water when the little guy comes out with Juke.

"He'll be fine," the little guy says. "It's a through and through. No other damage."

"It didn't hit nothin' that matters?"

"Keep the wounds covered and he'll be fine."

Tommy walks with Juke, shakes his head. "Five large for that," he says as the little guy steps around them to unlock the door. "Hey. My fuckin' pistol."

The little guy pulls it from a pocket, hands it to Tommy and lets them outside. "Oh, and these." Tommy and Juke are on the porch when the little guy opens his other hand and flings the pistol cartridges beyond them. He shuts the door as Tommy steps into the yard.

* * *

"You droppin' me at my place?" Juke asks.

They're a couple miles from the doc.

"A couple stops first. Gotta throw this piece." He pats his pistol, still unloaded. "Then we gotta see that asshole Karma. He got yours."

"That fuck?" Juke raises his eyebrows. "How'd he get it?"

"You dropped it, he picked it up. Gotta call him first, though. God knows where that motherfucker is."

Juke gets out his phone, punches in the number.

"You got that shit memorized?"

"Some names I don't want on my phone."

After a minute, Juke talks. "Yo, it's Juke. You got somethin' of mine. Call me, let's meet."

Tommy drives to water. Needs a spot that ain't crowded. There's plenty little walking bridges for that. He's headed toward one he knows near Laney College, near downtown. Won't be packed with students on a Saturday afternoon and he don't think there's a flea market in the parking lot this time of year. Don't matter much; he'll walk as far as he has to while Juke waits in the car.

Tommy pulls over just past the bridge, gets out, and in under a minute he's looking down at the water. It's running; there was actually rain this year. He looks side to side and the weather's nice enough but when people want a scenic view of water, they go another mile and they're at Lake Merritt. Here you're mostly on the edge of a junior college. Nobody around. Tommy gets his Ruger from his jacket but his first thought, to flip it underhand into the water, won't work unless he steps back and tosses it high. Bad idea if anyone drives past. An overhand throw same thing, about as obvious as you can get. He checks side to side again, looks back at the road. When there's no cars he holds his arm out and drops the pistol, pulls his arm back and watches his old weapon fall straight, no movement to it but down. It's in the water in an instant.

His hand returns to his pocket, makes sure he's got all six cartridges and brings out a fist. Which is all he holds out over the edge of the rail. The cartridges fall and he barely watches. Not nearly so sentimental about them. Fired a lot of rounds over the years. But he'll miss his Ruger. Scared men for a lot of years with that weapon. Hurt a few too.

Juke's dozing when Tommy gets back to the car. The doc shot him up with something for the pain. Had to cut into the arm around where the bullet hit to clear out any possible infection. After a night of sleeping on a floor, a few minutes in a motionless car must have been the nudge he needed to doze again. He breathes normal, that's all that matters. No driving with a dead man.

Another half hour and they're outside Juke's place. Nice building.

"Hey Juke."

No answer. The unwounded arm next to him, Tommy jostles Juke's shoulder. "Hey. We're here. Your place."

Juke's eyes flicker.

"Only I don't know how to get in the garage."

"Pull up to the gate."

Tommy rolls forward, stops this side of the gate, a garage entry box to his left. He looks at it but there's no way to pay.

Juke grimaces as he removes his wallet from his pants. He flips it open and removes a credit-card-sized piece of thick white plastic.

He holds it out to Tommy. "Flash the stripes at the sensor."

Tommy guesses, runs the card in front of the machine's grates. The bar keeping them out of the garage stays put. He moves the card up instead of down. Still nothing.

"Nah, the sensor. On the left."

The left side of the box is flat except where it curves out in a shape like it might dispense coins. He runs the card under that. The gate goes up.

"Take a left at the second row," Juke says. "I'm space seventeen."

Tommy rolls the car into the well-lit garage, takes a left at the second row and watches the space numbers.

"Almost all the way down. On the left."

"How the hell is number seventeen almost all the way down the second row?"

"I just live here, Tommy. I didn't number the fucking thing."

Tommy parks, helps Juke out, locks the car.

"I'm okay gettin' to my room," Juke says. "I'll give ya a twenty, cover your ride home. You know the address here?"

"Saw it pullin' in." Tommy takes the twenty Juke hands him. "I'll call a cab."

Juke grins. "You can walk out the garage the way we drove in."

"You got your ringer on? In case he calls back."

"Or a text. Sound on both."

"Good," Tommy says. "And another piece?"

Juke nods.

Tommy walks out the garage and calls a cab. He should go home and clean up—gotta be clean when he pays off Carelli—but there's something else he has to do first.

Good, Eddie's behind the bar.

"Jesus, Tommy." Eddie hands him a beer. "You been to bed this week?"

Tommy lays money on the bar. "Just busy. Hey, I need somethin' right away. Like, now."

Eddie shakes his head. "Work don't come like that."

"Got the work. Need a tool."

"Small?"

"Yeah, but not too light."

"Gimme a hour."

Tommy throws back half the beer. Man it's good right now. Feels early, but it ain't. Last night ran long. He takes the rest of the glass and sits at a table. Feels good to rest. Can't relax though. Not in a place he's met Karma. Sits a few minutes, finishes his beer, and walks out. Not sick anymore but sore all over.

Moves slow, walks along walls, eyes to the street. Hates being unarmed. Come up against Karma, he's gonna need a weapon. Hell, might need to shoot him in the back. That guy's good with a pistol. Too bad he's fucking insane.

It's mid-afternoon and the sun's at the height of its December powers, penetrates the chill but it's still cool out, light jacket weather. Tommy figures it's as warm as he's gonna feel until Karma's dead. His head's on a swivel; looks behind on the sidewalk, out to the street, straight ahead again. He needs a gun and he needs a shot, but no booze until after Karma and Carelli. He keeps track of the time and the streets, goes up one and turns, same thing again and again until it's been half an hour. Then it's back to Eddie on a cautious route that takes as long as the one here.

There's another guy behind the bar with Eddie now. Must be time for the night shift. Tommy steps to the bar.

Eddie's around it and walks him to the far side of the room. ".38 or .357?"

"What's the .38?"

"S and W."

"Let's see it."

Eddie steps into the parking lot and Tommy follows.

Ain't a Ruger but it'll do. A snubnose, it fits in his shoulder holster. Tommy wants to go home and change but maybe there ain't time. Maybe he just smells like shit today. He got Karma to deal with, gotta get Carelli over with so that don't become a deal too. His car still at the house, he gets out his phone and calls another cab, heads down by the lake.

Carelli's at his usual Starbucks table, a newspaper in front of him but he ain't looking at it.

"Hey," Tommy says. He sits. "Got what I owe. You want it here?"

Carelli shakes his head, stands. "We walk."

"I got it," Tommy says, half a block down the street, "but it ain't in a envelope or anything."

"Jesus." Carelli walks beside him. "You a moron? Just gonna hand me five large on a sidewalk?"

Tommy's surprised. "I dunno, man, thought you'd have a place you do things like this."

"Yeah, the place is called the sidewalk. And the guy hands me a fuckin' bag or somethin', maybe a box with a ribbon on it like it's a present if he's smart. Didn't expect that from you, ain't a lotta smart guys out there, but stupid? You want a fuckin' crown for it?"

"I just wanna pay you. It didn't go perfect, I want the money end done. Last night—"

Carelli reaches up and grabs Tommy by the shoulders, shakes him. "I don't give a fuck about last night." Keeps his voice low. "You owe me, you pay me. Shut the fuck up."

Carelli lets go, Tommy steps forward. He watches, makes sure Carelli steps with him. "Sorry. Just wanna get straight with you. That's all this is. Where?"

Carelli puts a hand in his lower back, pushes him forward. "I tell you where to turn, you go with me. I'm gonna take your money in a men's room. And I ain't gonna see you again."

They take a right at the corner, another right at the Grand Lake Theatre. Neither says a word, they just walk down Grand. Every step Tommy takes feels like two. Maybe he dies tonight. Carelli don't seem like a killer but what the fuck's going on? Everything's a restaurant and they walk past every restaurant. There's also a local clothes place and a whiskey shop and a bookstore that takes up more space than makes sense. Back to the restaurants soon enough and Tommy still has this feeling he's gonna die. But in a restaurant? Why? Stupid don't get a man killed or there'd be nothing but corpses.

Carelli turns in front of a sandwich board, walks into a Mexican place. Tommy follows.

Twenty feet inside, Carelli says, "Hey, Connie," to the woman behind the counter and keeps walking.

She looks sixty and tired, throws on a smile and says "Hi," but Carelli's down the back and Tommy follows.

Carelli waits at a bathroom door, pushes it open for Tommy and steps in behind him, locks the door.

Carelli holds a .45 aimed at Tommy's chest. "Where's the fuckin' money?"

Tommy pats his coat.

"And your piece? Show me."

Tommy opens up the other side of his coat, shows the .38 in his shoulder holster.

Carelli nods and Tommy shuts his coat. "Gimme the money. Reach the wrong way and Connie got a mess to clean."

CHAPTER TWELVE

Tommy goes home. It's about time for dinner and past time for a shower and a change of clothes. No way to stay clean wearing these. And he's going back out soon as he hears from Juke. If Karma causes trouble, best if there's two of them.

No one at the house but Rommel, who greets Tommy at the door like he's eager for a walk. "You fuckin' dog." Tommy smiles. "We walked all night."

Not enough for the dog, Tommy knows, but plenty for him. Any walk Rommel gets tonight will be with Malik. And it's Saturday night—see if the teenager's even home before dark. Tommy just needs to get clean. And some sleep. Best he can hope for while he's here.

He washes thoroughly in the shower, a fresh pint of bourbon on the side for sipping and Christ he needs it, knows a lot of his shit drains down the tub. He's been gross and he won't be when he changes into the clean clothes he laid across the bathroom counter. He gets out, dries best he can, and puts them on. Quiet when he steps into the hall. He listens for sounds in the kitchen. Nothing.

Pushes the bedroom door open, leaves it that way, and plops onto the bed. His phone and whiskey on the little table next to his head, ready for Juke's call, but really he waits for Carla. Blinks rapidly each second he waits. Didn't even know he'd dozed when he feels her shaking him.

"Get up."

He stands half awake, grabs his pillow to take to the living room.

She grabs it too. "They got pillows in motels."

"Wha—? The floor."

"You blew your floor probation, Tommy. Get outta here. This is my place. Me and my family."

He knows better than to argue. Not now. He comes back sober with the money, then they can talk. For now, she's gonna win no matter what. He grabs a pair of socks and looks around for his shoes. She has to be watching him and she wants him out, has to know what he's looking for and don't say a word. He walks out of the room.

Checks the bathroom floor, nothing there either. Back to the living room, awake enough now to feel his head bursting. The rest of him feels okay, at least not as bad as his head. His shoes on the floor in front of the couch where Rommel lies, he sits beside his dog and pets him but he's just comforting himself and knows it, puts his shoes on. Leans back on the couch, sees the bloodstain, has to be Juke's. Tries to remember where his jacket is, the money still inside. He wakes up a little more, picks up the jacket where it's draped over the back of the couch. His hand had been resting on it. The shoulder holster with the S&W .38 underneath. Jesus, he forgot. Puts on the holster then the jacket and walks out the door. It ain't late and his body ain't killing him and he could use a drink. Just one or two, Juke could call any time about Karma. He drives with windows down, takes in the brisk air to wake up and decides which hotel he'd like tonight.

"He's like a pit bull with clipped ears," Juke says. "Ain't gotta bark. Just watches and he's a good watchdog."

Tommy nods. He's got his bourbon but he can't remember the name of Eddie's night bartender. Weird how some guys stay strangers no matter how many times they serve you. At least they're at the bar, he can always flag him down. Looks at Juke. "And he don't call."

"I worry he got somethin' in mind."

"He ain't in with Keene, right? I know he ain't with Lee."

"Nah," Juke says. "He is one indie motherfucker."

"You know Carelli?"

"Who he is, sure. Never met the man. You in with him?"

"Done business with him. I guarantee he knows about Karma." Tommy drinks. "He's gonna charge. Less if *you* go."

Juke grins, winces, shakes his head.

"Your arm?"

"It's nothin'." He drinks his scotch.

Tommy's already waving for another drink.

"So, you pissed off Carelli?"

Tommy's eyes stay focused on the bartender. "Not forever, but I don't wanna drive up the price."

Juke nods. "You pissed off Carelli. He still at the same Starbucks?"

"Like he was born at that table."

***

Juke's with Carelli, Tommy's not. Nah, he's in this fucking rented room and he don't know how long, with his gun and his money and he'll use one to keep the other. So it's a lot better than the really cheap rooms, hell this one's kind of nice and no way he'd have it except for the cash. The goddamn cash. Get ripped off in one of the cheap joints he usually crashes in and this whole fucking thing collapses, including the deal where he winds up home with the money and Carla takes him back when she sees he got his shit together. So he waits for Juke to finish with Carelli. Of course Carelli's gonna know Juke's his partner, so he might charge extra for that, but it won't be what he'd charge if it was Tommy in person. He hopes.

This room's comfortable, he ain't. And he knows what he's spending and he don't like it. But he knows what a cheap motel door is like, how easy a random crew could show up and take everything in his coat and maybe kill him because they can. Fucking amateurs everywhere. So he's here and it's safe. He pays extra for safety and he knows it's where he has to be. And Juke's gonna find out where Karma is, and they're gonna have to step up to that crazy motherfucker, and no way that's easy. He's gonna want Carla after and she ain't gonna be there.

He checks his phone. No messages, no missed calls, ringer turned up all the way. Fucker better call soon. If they gotta lay this asshole to waste he wants a victory drink as soon as possible.

TV's on but nothing's on, no sports he gives a fuck about and no movies except the kind with pretty people. He hates pretty people. Fake ones on a screen anyway. Pretty women in real life? A whole other kind of problem, but every man's life has problems.

So the news is on, but if there's anything about the robbery and the murders he ain't seen it. More phonies smiling at each other no matter what they say. Best thing about the news in Oakland—murders don't rate as a surprise, maybe get mentioned but then it's on to the latest scandal, government or cops or whoever's next in line.

Tommy walks down one end of the room and back, doing laps, looks at the screen sometimes but there's never anything to see.

His phone rings. He removes it from his pocket, don't know how long he's been here.

It's Juke. "I got an address."

"I'm in a room downtown, for the night at least. That on your way or do I meetcha there?"

"I get you. One car's best."

A safe in the closet. Tommy locked the money in there a while ago, which was one thing, but now he leaves the room and that's a whole other. There's a safe in every closet in this hotel, no reason anyone would target *him*. He sure as hell don't look like a guy with money.

He won't wait in the lobby; being indoors is driving him fucking nuts. He don't know what Karma's up to, don't even know if Karma knows. Only knows they can't leave his place without Juke's piece.

A pickup area out front. Tommy paces, waits for Juke. Has his new pistol, don't want to use it. Already in all those murders at The Manatee, don't want to do one on his own and maybe get caught this time. Hell, if any of them get tied to The Manatee they're all murder one. Fuck this. He paces, wants a drink, needs to get this

Karma business over with.

The pacing goes on forever. Finally Juke pulls up. Tommy gets in and they drive. He sits back, fidgets, moves forward in his seat and clenches his fists, looks at Juke. "Carelli give up anything besides the address?"

Juke shakes his head. "Says Karma's a loner. He hates that about him, makes it hard to get info. But everyone makes a mistake. One mistake and Carelli knows where you live."

"And once he knows he knows forever. Bastard knows my real last name, everything about me ever made the paper." He laughs. "Carelli still reads papers, knows shit. Talks to people, knows more. If he got a computer, he don't bring it to work."

"Shakes ain't your real name?"

"Shakes ain't no one's real name."

"He said somethin' else, Tommy. You been seein' some chick?"

"What about it?"

"Carelli says her husband works for Joey Lee."

"Fuck."

"Yeah, it cost extra to find that out."

"Fuck. That all you could get?"

"Couldn't afford more. You owe me."

They shut up awhile. Until they get close to Karma's and Juke makes a left. "It's this street. Twenty-three eighty-eight. Watch for it." He drives slow.

"House or apartment?"

"Apartment. Should be first floor. Number eleven."

"Slow down. Hard to see numbers at night."

Juke slows way the fuck down. They both look, neither talks. No other cars on the street right now. Juke still watches the road.

"That building ahead," Tommy says. "Has to be."

He points but Juke's eyes are on it. No parking this side of the street, he swings a sudden U and parallels into a tight space. Both men get out of the car and cross the street.

It's a few steps up from the sidewalk to the building's front door. Juke presses the buzzer for eleven, D'Angelo.

"Hey Karma, it's Juke and Tommy. We brought booze."

The front door buzzes. Tommy pushes it open. "Surprised the fuck has his own name on the door."

Juke takes a quick look to the left. "And it's the first door. Guess he don't expect no one to find him."

"No one he's afraid of." Tommy says it soft, steps to the far side of the door. Juke stops on the near side. Neither will be in view when the door opens. Tommy knocks twice, hard.

"It's open!" Karma hollers.

Tommy shakes his head in case Juke's suddenly stupid.

"Nah," Tommy says. "You open it."

It takes a minute but Karma opens the door wide, sees both men. "Fuck," Karma says, "it's cool." He turns around and walks straight back, sits behind a fold-up card table on the near end of a couch that faces the door. "Gotcha glasses." He points to three on the table.

Tommy enters the room slow, Juke behind him. "You act all trustin' for a guy with a couch faces the door."

"We're the same side," Karma says. Then to Juke, just inside the door, "Shut that. And bolt it. Anyone maybe picks that lock. That fuckin' bolt? Gotta be a goddamn specialist."

Juke gets the door bolted and Tommy sits next to Karma. Juke sits next to Tommy.

"Big fuckin' couch," Tommy says.

"You ain't shittin' 'bout that drink, right?" Karma says. "I could use one."

"Inside my coat. Want me to open it first?"

"Just get the fuckin' bottle out. Jesus."

Tommy uncorks the bottle, fills each glass, the bottle almost empty after that.

Karma raises an eyebrow. "Ain't gonna be much of a drinkin' party."

Juke pats the top of his glass. "Gimme my pistol you can have my fuckin' drink."

Karma drinks from his own glass, sets it down. "It's good, but one drink or two, ain't hardly a party either way." He looks at Juke. "Ain't got your pistol."

"You picked it up."

"I know guys get you a new one, but I didn't bring no pistols home."

"Wasn't my only pistol."

"You gonna show me the new one? Then I show you what I got, only someone get the wrong idea, it gets fuckin' messy in here. And I gotta clean up."

"Ain't here for bullshit." Juke picks up his glass left-handed. His voice barely above a whisper. "Just my pistol."

"Now Karma," Tommy cuts in, "we seen what a badass you are with a gun. Don't forget, Juke saved your ass. Man just wants his piece back."

"So you know I'm good with a handgun," Karma says. "You think I got this good without a lotta practice? You think that fuckin' practice was all on a fuckin' range? Jobs, boy. A lotta jobs. One where a piece comes home?" Karma shakes his head. "Never. Now, we gonna drink or what?"

Tommy looks at Juke.

Juke's eyes stay on Karma. "There's also my arm. Cost money to patch it up, and the way I got it...ain't none of us gets away from there I don't do that."

"All for one. Whadda I owe?"

"Twelve-fifty."

"Need help findin' the other motherfucker?"

"I can find him," Tommy says. "You might help convince."

"I pay you tonight, tomorrow good for him? Just, we should get another bottle. Good shit."

"Fine. Don't need you tomorrow though. Don't want Dunbar thinkin' we goin' strongarm on him."

"Yeah," Karma says, "you ain't got Juke goin' alone though, do ya?"

"He would with a good right shoulder. I trust Dunbar. Don't mean we play this stupid."

They'd barely opened the second fifth when Juke left, things to do besides drink. Tommy and Karma, not so much. Didn't finish the fifth but close enough, each of them looking over the edge of their glass at the other as they drank. Suspicious, no trust, that was the problem; people talk about honor among thieves but no way Tommy is letting his guard down around this crazy motherfucker. They drink all night though.

Next morning he wakes in the hotel, head throbbing and back tight. He lies there awhile getting used to the pain, gets up slow and makes coffee. Glad the only person he has to meet today is Dunbar. That can wait until he talks to Juke. It's Juke's money they're collecting, and no way Dunbar argues one against two.

Tommy takes his coffee, finds the remote, finds ESPN. Football talk, good. He likes professional violence. Fucking fag rules these days, protect the overpaid cock-suckers. Best highlights are still when someone takes someone's head off.

Coffee's hot, football talk's pointless, just show the highlights. No one on the Niners is any good anymore, not like when Eddie D. ran the show. Or even when they gave Harbaugh control a couple years, before Bowman's brutal leg break and Willis and The Cowboy retired. Tommy hates it all, wants revenge on everyone, the strangers who wrecked his Sundays. Revenge on Carla, but not exactly *on* her. Just she kicked him out, set Malik against him. She can't see she's wrong, he'll take it out wherever he can. Not right now, though. For now everything's smooth; he has money, just lost what he got it for.

He finishes two coffees, makes a call and Juke comes by. Tommy can drive to Dunbar's, let Juke's wound heal. Don't expect any need for a fast getaway. If he did, Juke would drive and fuck healing.

The Double O has a small parking lot but there's a space and Tommy takes it. He and Juke go inside, get a table and order beers. Dunbar wouldn't give up his address but Tommy told him how much money to bring.

It's a table for four. Raiders gear hangs everywhere, uniforms and helmets and championship banners. All that shit's old, looks it. Tommy and Juke have seats that face the door. They're halfway through their pints when Dunbar walks in, looks around the room a minute. Tommy waves and he joins them.

"We got a waitress?"

Tommy nods and Dunbar sits.

Rob Pierce

"You brought the money?" Tommy asks.

"Why I'm here. Takes two to collect money that's just for him?"

"Two's insurance Juke gets paid. You want a business where there's trust about money? Good fuckin' luck."

"Money's in a envelope in my pocket. Can pass it to Juke any time. Where's the waitress? We in a fuckin' bar, right?"

"She might show faster if we bought more than two beers. What's the tip on that?"

"Where is she?"

Tommy points.

Dunbar stands, pulls a bill from his wallet, waves at her, whistles like he's calling a cab and hollers: "Hey honey, good money for some drinks over here!"

Tommy's hands cover his face and he shakes his head.

She comes over quick, a paunchy brunette, face looks like she's gone a few rounds.

Dunbar still stands, hands her a twenty. "That's for you. These boys pay for these?"

She nods, looks at the bill a moment then wads it in her fist, shoves it into her apron.

"And your best whiskey all around, plus another beer for these two whatever they had, and one of whatever those two had for me."

"They had different beers."

"Gimme one of each."

Tommy's hands came off his face when the waitress reached their table. Now he leans back, eyes wide at Dunbar, voice soft. "What the fuck was that? We don't want attention."

"*That*," Dunbar says, "is getting a waitress for life. I tip good again this round, you think she ever says a

167

word against me? But she remembers me. That's *my* insurance."

What worries Tommy now is who's gonna crack when the cops show? A job like this goes wrong, that's how it always happens. He's sure Juke'll stand up, but he don't know Karma or Dunbar. Fuck it was stupid bringing those guys in. Better get ready to blow town fast first time something looks funny. Throw whatever shit he wants to take in his car.

Another reason to see Carla. He likes his other reasons better but they ain't gonna happen tonight. Tonight he don't wanna stay alone. Calls Amanda, asks if she wants to meet him for a drink.

"What, now you're ready to use me again?"

"What's it been, a week?"

"Try two."

Tommy's in his room, gotta get out. Hell, gotta move out, fuckin' pricey by the night. Another thing ain't gonna happen before tomorrow. "You wanted this casual and I been busy. Sounds perfect to me."

"I never said casual. I don't fuck casual."

"No you don't. Now it sounds like you got a temper too."

"You say that like you're smilin'." Didn't sound like *she* was.

"You wanna see me smile, lemme buy ya a drink."

"You're an asshole, Tommy."

"I'll be at Jacks or Better." He ends the call.

Half an hour and he's there. She ain't. He orders a beer

and a shot, drinks at a table and waits for her. She shows or she don't. Either way he's better off than sitting in that hotel room. Ain't gonna meet no other broads if she don't show, not in this dump.

Busy in here tonight, Monday Night Football on two screens behind the bar. Gives him something to look at while he drinks but his mind's on other shit. Still, he enjoys the brutal hits, wishes they showed more line play and less of these candy-ass "skill" players. Fucking game's indoors too, no snow, no mud, no weather at all. Anyone ends a football game in a clean uniform's a bench warmer or a pussy.

Game's close, fourth quarter—still early here but the game's back east—and Tampa's across midfield. Winston drops back, has time, throws a bullet over the middle, open receiver but a safety comes out of nowhere, drills him and the ball pops loose, incomplete.

"Wooh!" Tommy yells. He don't care who wins but that was a great hit. Then the TV shows a ref, a flag on the ground, and he signals personal foul. On that? That *is* football. "Make 'em play in skirts," Tommy grumbles.

"You don't like skirts?" Amanda stands behind him.

"I like you in 'em. And out." He stands. "Let's get you a drink."

They walk to the bar together, his drinks still on the table. He'll fuckin' kill anyone who takes 'em and no way that don't show. Men are lined up behind the men on barstools, couldn't order fast before and now it's late in the game it's gonna be harder.

He waves her back but she stands close. He leans between guys got seats, neither seems to notice when he bumps against them. Drunks into the game. He waves at the bartender, keeps waving until he gets a nod. He's been seen but football fans drink. Tommy should get faster service than the ones who don't tip, but they get drunk enough he bets the bartender gets extra money somehow. It takes a few minutes then Tommy gets two beers and two bourbons neat, hands the bottles to Amanda and walks back to the table with her.

"I'm not a beer drinker," she says as they sit.

He sets the bourbon glasses in front of her. "Take these. Good shit."

"You coulda asked what I want."

"You showed up. I know what you want."

She looks around his room. "Nicer than before."

"Ain't stayin'," Tommy says. "And it ain't where the millionaires stay. But yeah, for how long I'm here? I can do this."

"Wish you were here longer."

She says it soft but he throws a smile her way. "After the next job." He pulls the blade from his pants, cuts through the bottle's plastic seal and uncorks it. Takes a swig and passes it to her.

She drinks. "You get good stuff, Tommy."

"Why drink if you don't know what's good?" He takes the bottle back, drinks again, turns so she backs up closer to the bed.

She puts a hand behind his back and he swats her arm.

She backs up, he steps forward. The dance continues until she bumps against the bed. She smooths the front of her skirt, steps out of her shoes, and falls back graceful as she can.

CHAPTER THIRTEEN

Tommy wakes, Amanda next to him. Mild hangover and his gut ain't sending him into spasms so he figures last night went alright. He gets out of bed slow, boils enough water for at least two coffees and that's just for him, gets his cup and filter set up and worries there's a double-cross coming. Don't know Dunbar or Karma. He should take out both but Karma'd likely kill him. And if he takes out Dunbar without talking to Karma first, Karma might figure he's next. And he can't talk to Karma first, don't know if he can trust the motherfucker. So if he kills either, it's Karma first.

He pours his coffee. Jesus. Juke's the one guy on the deal he knows he can trust and Juke's the guy gave him Karma's number. If he's gonna start shooting people he oughta start with himself for trusting Juke. He shakes his head, half a grin. "How this gonna go down?" he says, barely audible.

"You talkin' to your coffee?"

Tommy looks over his shoulder. Amanda stood behind him. "Didn't know I was talkin'."

"You were."

He gets another cup from the cabinet, puts a couple scoops of coffee in the filter and pours.

He drinks, looks at her. "You ain't got much on. Looks good on you."

"You either."

"And?"

"You're okay." She gives a little grin.

"How awake are you?" He steps toward her.

"What do you have in mind?"

"Who I gotta worry about?" His hands on her shoulders.

She steps back. He don't let go. He shakes her. "Who?"

She leans forward. "I don't know, Tommy."

He pushes and she staggers away. "Let's go see your husband. Got a feeling he's Chinese."

"What? Whatta you care what he is?"

"Don't care what he is. What I care's who he is. Who he works for."

"We can't go there."

Tommy watches her. She barely moves as he puts on his shoulder holster, his jacket. "We go there together," Tommy walks up to the dresser, grabs socks from a drawer, "who's he shoot first?"

She doesn't answer. He walks backward and sits on the bed, puts on his socks and shoes. "Get dressed."

"You ain't kiddin'? Tommy, you're gonna wreck my marriage."

"Your marriage or my life. Let's go."

Her car's a shining silver Lexus. "Someone's takin' care of you." Tommy gets in.

"I paid for it." Amanda starts the car, pulls into the street.

"With money?" Tommy's heard this talk before. "Or sacrifices?"

"You're gonna fuckin' kill me, Tommy."

"Tell me his name, maybe we skip the trip."

"I can say his name. You won't know him." She drives slow. "What do you want to know?"

"His name. Speed up."

She takes the Lexus up to the speed limit.

"Waste of a machine, drivin' this slow. You ever air it out?"

She shakes her head fast. "Not now, Tommy."

"You sound sad. Wanna leave his name out? Who's he work for?"

"Lexus."

Tommy laughs. "He sells cars? He cut you a deal?"

"I married him," her voice angry, afraid. "That's no deal."

"Nice car, though. For a salesman's wife."

"He's sales *manager*."

"So he *really* got a deal on this. Nice."

"The money's good. I been in your car."

"Fuck you, Amanda. How'd he get that job? And why don't he care you stay out all night?"

"He was good at sales. He can't keep me home."

"And he don't knock you around? Don't sound like a man works for Joey Lee."

"Wha—? Joey who?" She sounds surprised, not ignorant.

"You know who Joey is? Regular people don't."

"Joey who? That's what I said."

"Heard ya say it. Heard how ya said it. Joey ain't your husband, I know that much. Man like that don't need a wife. Someone works for him? Yeah, that's who we gonna see."

"You can't see him." She sounds about to cry.

He reaches in her purse, digs around and flips one thing after another onto the floor, pulls out her driver's license. "We're goin' to this address. He's home, we see him. Or you answer my questions, maybe this waits."

"Who he works for?"

"That's a start."

"Lexus."

"Keep drivin'."

Her grip tight on the wheel, her shoulders tight. "The guy who hired him? That help?"

"Maybe."

"This guy came to the house. I thought that was funny. And he wasn't in a suit. Green fatigue jacket over a black shirt. Looked like he'd been working out and was showing off."

"You thought he was hot?"

"Someone would. Tall, muscular, black."

"You get a name?"

"Yeah. I answered the door then he was off in a room with my husband."

"Gimme a name, Amanda." Ready to throw her through a window.

"Mister Wolf, he said."

"Taurean Wolf?"

"I didn't catch his first name."

Tommy nods. "Your husband ain't Chinese, is he? He's black."

"What?"

"He's black. You're gonna tell me his name."

"I can't."

"He kill you if you do? What the fuck's he do when

you bring me to him?"

"No."

"Bad answer. Word got out on this job I was doin'. I changed up the night but the guys who knew ahead? Showed up, but too late to fuck with things. You was a damn good spy, honey. Who's Taurean's boss? Percelle's? Rashad's?"

Her face changes as she drives. "I only met Mister Wolf once."

"Your story's bullshit. Wolf meets your husband at his house, it ain't a job offer. Wolf works for him, and those other names? Bangers, every one. Dead now, nothin' to do with me but your old man thinks so? We're goin' to him. Tell me his name. He's black, right?"

She drives, nods fast, he thinks she gulps but her eyes stay on the road and her long hair fucks with his view of her neck.

"He's black," Tommy says again.

She gulps for sure this time. "Yeah." The word barely comes out.

"And he knew those guys."

He waits a minute, she don't answer. "Those dead guys."

"He—he knew them."

The road's dark. They've been on it several minutes, no cars either direction. "Pull over."

"Why?" She drives straight.

"We gonna talk. You gonna live."

She keeps driving but he said the reason and he don't even need to give a fuckin' reason. "Pull. Over."

The street ain't wide but it ain't tight curves either and parking on the shoulder ain't dangerous unless two cars show up going opposite directions on this road where they ain't even seen one.

She eases up on the gas, guides the car to the side. "What?"

"What? You ain't answered a goddamn question, that's what. Your husband's name, who he works for, how's he know the dead guys?"

"You never cared about me."

Tommy smiles. "That goes both ways. Only I was never full of shit."

"What?" Her eyes go wide. "I never lied to you."

"Your husband's name, bitch."

"His name's Von."

"First name or last?"

"Von Parker."

"See how easy that is? Now, how's Von know the dead guys?"

"They—they worked together."

"For who?"

"I don't know."

"Better find out. While we're parked here."

She undoes her seatbelt, turns, and faces him. "Von took a lot of private calls."

"You trying to die, Amanda?"

Her teeth grit. "You could kill me, Tommy?"

He puts both hands behind her neck, thumbs tight on her throat.

"Who's Von work for?"

"He never talks work. Says the dealership is dull."

"But you know he don't do shit for Lexus."

She nods. "Doesn't make sense if he does. The guys he meets dress like you."

"And Von dresses how?"

"Suits, ties. He's a businessman."

"But you don't know what business."

She coughs. "Let go of my neck?"

Tommy smiles, loosens his grip. "Too tight. I was getting used to it."

She coughs some more.

"He's a front," Tommy says.

"A front?"

"Man between the dirt and the real money. Fuckin' pussy job."

"Because he doesn't hurt people?"

"Don't kid yourself," Tommy says. "No one gets hurt someone don't do what he does. He's a fence or something. No one kills for the money if they don't get the money. He got one of those jobs gets killers paid."

Amanda shivers.

"Don't wanna hear it? You know I'm right. Now, who's your killer husband work for?"

"He doesn't say."

"He meet with anyone besides those guys?"

She shakes her head. Now the shiver accompanies the headshake.

"Ever talk about his boss at Lexus?"

"Not really."

"Say a name."

He leans toward her.

She jerks her head back and they almost bump foreheads. "Joey. He's a regional manager or something, doesn't talk to Von. But when Von's stressed, that's who he blames. Fucking Joey, he says."

Tommy falls back in his seat, holds his chest like it might explode. Joey Lee might not know about The Manatee but his hands are in something else these guys are doing. This is all gonna blow up in Tommy's face.

Or maybe—he feels like he's dreaming—it all blows up in Von's.

He kisses the top of her head. "Take us to your place. We get to the top of the driveway, turn the fuckin' car around."

They get there and sit long enough for Tommy to check the place out. It's a nice-looking house but not that far back from the street, not like a rich person's. Not that kind of spread, just a normal yard, grass and a tree, a front porch bigger than most, a few chairs on it.

"Write that down for me," he says.

"What?"

"Your address."

"Like, text it to you?"

"No!" His face in hers. "I don't want that shit on my phone."

She gulps. "What? What are you gonna do, Tommy?"

"I ain't doin' shit. Don't want shit to do with your old man is all. Not him, not the guys he works for."

"Joey."

"Just write it down," he says.

"With what? On what?"

"A pen. Paper. Whaddaya think?"

"I don't have those," she says. "I have a phone."

"Jesus." He tips his head back. "Turn the fuckin' car around."

She checks for traffic, backs up the car and swings a wide U. "Where we goin'?"

"Back where we were," Tommy says.

"The bar?"

"I parked outside."

She drives. Neither of them talks. She reaches for the radio.

"Leave it."

They're quiet, the only sound the cool air blowing through her open window. His stays shut. She glances at him, he watches the road.

A few miles down he points at a gas station. "Pull in. We go inside together."

She parks off to the side, away from the gas tanks. Not exactly a mini-mart but he puts his arm around her and they walk to the beers. He grabs a six-pack, stops on the way to the register and grabs a can of Coke, then a napkin from next to the microwave. Sets everything on the counter, gets a twenty from his wallet while the cashier, an Arabic man probably in his twenties, rings him up. "Hey boss, got a pen? Just for a second."

"You pay cash?"

Tommy holds up the twenty.

"Fourteen fifty."

Tommy pays. The cashier gives him his change then the pen. Tommy pulls Amanda closer to him and the napkin. She writes fast. He looks, makes sure he can read it, folds it inside the bills and puts them all in his wallet.

Another minute and they're back in the car, on the road in two. It's a winding highway, damn near a freeway. She drives—fast, sure, ignoring the brick barrier on her right—without looking at him.

"That first night," he says, halfway to his car, a few miles from where they'll return to surface streets, "how'd you know I was there? Who sent you?"

"I was there. *You* joined *me*."

"So you knew my local dive. Why?"

"I wanted a drink. A few. I was down that way. I go places remind me of where I grew up."

"Von send you?"

"I don't love him anymore."

"You still obey him."

"No."

"Someone told you go there, told you what I look like, told you leave with me. Von or someone else?"

"No one. I was just there."

"How many nights you go there before I showed? What were you supposed to get from me?"

"It wasn't like that."

"What's it like?"

"I have a shitty day and I drink. Had one that day. You showed that night."

Tommy shakes his head. "You are fuckin' good at lyin'."

"What can I tell you, Tommy? To make you believe me?"

"Hell, girl. You gotta make me believe this just happened. That the broad I meet in that bar that night, a bar where I'm a regular, first time I see her *and* I hook up with her, turns out her old man works with some guys tried to fuck with me. Why would a guy like me trust a pretty girl? What kinda idiot I gotta be to buy that? Now, you can tell me that's bullshit. Don't know what fuckin' happens if you do, only you're better off tellin' the truth."

She's almost in tears. "I told you the truth."

He slaps her across the face and her hands drop, the car swerves. He grabs the wheel with one hand, straightens the car.

"You think Von's gonna hurt you? He ain't here. I am. That motherfucker ain't even in the picture much longer. Take the wheel. Drive. And tell me the fuckin' truth."

She drives again, don't talk.

"Only way this makes sense, someone in my crew talked. But why give yourself away?" He shakes his head. "Or someone *was* in my crew. You know a skinny white fuck name a Smallwood? A guy who acted like a pro but had a tweaker's heart? Five to one that motherfucker sold me out."

"Maybe. Hard to say. I don't know names. Don't wanna know. Lotta skinny white dudes come through."

"Clingin' to a life raft, honey? I need to know it was him or wasn't. What do you know? It's your raft. Don't drown."

"He. He maybe came by the house a couple times."

"When?"

"This month, I think."

After I kicked him off the job, Tommy figures. "You hear anything?"

"He's seein' Von, I ain't supposed to listen after that."

"But you hear things."

"Can't be sure what he said."

"You spy on your husband. You're pretty damn sure."

She watches the freeway signs, like she's unsure of her off-ramp.

"Sounded like," she says, "there's a job. That's the white guy talking. Then he says, some of your guys might be interested. And he says the name of the place. I don't remember. And he says Joey has a guy in it but Joey doesn't know."

"This is before you met me."

"I guess."

"And all this time Von's scared of a guy named Joey and you know Joey Lee and you don't put two and two together."

"I don't *know* Joey Lee."

181

"You know who he is."

She nods.

"You got a cute little nose. Some doctor did a good job."

"What?"

"You Pinocchio, honey. He cut it way shorter."

"Fuck you, Tommy."

"That prick Smallwood tried to get me killed."

"I don't know about that." She's at the off-ramp.

He puts an arm around her. "It's when you started seeing me. It's why. Smallwood sold me out to Von. You did what Von said because he scares you. I get that. What you gotta get now? And I mean fuckin' right now? Your old man crossed Joey Lee. Von's dead. We don't have to be, you tell me everything you know."

"Von's dead?"

"Keep the fuckin' car straight. Joey finds out, he's dead. Joey's gonna find out."

"Joey finds out what?"

"The place I took. Got no protection, but a guy works for Joey knows the joint. Why don't Joey know? That's how he thinks. Anyone works for him knows he thinks that way. It's fucked. Someone gonna die. Ain't me."

"I don't wanna know this shit."

"Bullshit. You spied on your husband so you'd know this shit."

"Not these details."

"Yeah. You wanted to get dirty and look clean. Fuck you, Amanda."

"Tommy. Von's my ex, we just live together. I'm always here for you."

"So," Tommy says, "he's out, I'm in?"

"It goes that way, it goes that way."

"You're a shitty person to count on."

"It's a shitty business. I thought I married a guy who worked for Lexus."

"He didn't tell you."

"Still hasn't."

Tommy nods. "I wanna fuck you so bad it hurts. Gotta talk to some guys first."

His car has a ticket on the windshield when she pulls up where he left it, near Jacks or Better. "Find parking. You're goin' with me."

"To talk to some guys?"

"You won't talk. Park."

"Don't hurt me, Tommy. Please."

He smiles wide. "Don't wanna fuck the wounded. Relax. Park."

She drives slow, takes a place a block away. They get out, walk to Tommy's car, his arm around her. Maybe they look like a couple.

Tommy walks her to the passenger side, lets her in the shotgun seat. He gets behind the wheel.

"What are we doing? Why am I with you for this?"

"We go to a bar. My friend there works nights sometimes. We see him, I talk. You keep your fuckin' mouth shut. Don't even say hi. This man don't wanna know. Of course, he knows you? We got somethin' to talk about."

"I don't know shit about Von's business."

"We gonna see."

CHAPTER FOURTEEN

They pull into the lot at Eddie's. Tommy walks Amanda through the front door. No seats at the bar but Eddie's serving drinks. Tommy's got Amanda by the hand, tight, walks her to one end of the bar and waves to Eddie. There's no one at the tables behind them. It's just a question of carrying their drinks over there.

"Hey," Tommy says when Eddie comes over. "You got a minute?"

"Not *this* minute. You drinkin'?"

"Two bourbons and a beer."

Eddie turns around, knows Tommy's brands, comes back with three glasses. "Guess you love birds gotta let go each other."

Tommy's money is already on the bar. He waits for the change, leaves a five for Eddie, turns to Amanda. "You carry the bourbons. That table on the wall." He aims his chin across the room, away from the door. They walk and sit.

Tommy raises his glass of beer. "Keep yer fuckin' mouth shut when Eddie gets here."

She gets a head start on that, takes a drink and don't say a word. Tommy sips his beer. He bought one of those bourbons for himself but he can see it's gonna be hers. The people at the bar are loud, the jukebox boring, the rest of the room empty.

Finally Eddie comes over. "Take the next seat," he says to Tommy. "I gotta watch the bar."

Tommy moves, Eddie sits. "What?"

"The Manatee," Tommy says. "Hear about it?"

"Armed robbery with a lotta guys dead? It mighta made the news."

Tommy nods. "Can you get word to Joey Lee?"

"I look Chinese to you?"

"But you can put it out where he's gonna hear it."

Eddie shrugs. "He hears what he hears."

"A guy Joey knows was behind it."

"You tellin' me with the broad here?" He shakes his head.

"Her husband," Tommy says. "Von something." He glares at Amanda. She keeps her mouth shut. He pulls out his wallet, finds the address, hands it to Eddie. "Von Parker. This is where he lives."

"That it?"

"For here, yeah."

Eddie stands, talks quiet. "What the fuck's in it for you, Tommy?"

"Joey's gratitude would be nice."

"And you get the broad?"

"Already got the broad."

Eddie bends down, his face in Tommy's, talks even softer. "What's in it for me?"

"A lot, we do this right. You got time tomorrow?"

"Early. I call you."

Tommy and Amanda at the hotel: it's night, they drink,

her in a chair across from the bed, him walking one end of the room to the other. One tall glass for each, the only two glasses he owns. He also has two coffee cups. Optimistic bastard. Twenty minutes, no words.

"Tomorrow," she says, and he stops. "You're telling him more, right? About Von?"

"Don't know much more."

"Then what?"

He drinks, lowers his glass, takes a step toward her. "Stuff that helps me. Helps him. Got nothin' to do with you."

"But I wanna know."

"You don't." He shakes his head, keeps stepping toward her. "You really don't."

He takes her by the shoulders, stands her up, turns to kiss her.

She walks away.

He grabs the bottle from the table and refills his glass.

Tommy's phone rings. Morning. Fuck. He's in bed, in a T-shirt and shorts, Amanda fully clothed beside him. His head throbs. He wakes, picks up the call. "Yeah?"

"At the bar. Now." It's Eddie.

"Yeah."

Tommy's out of bed, Amanda don't stir. He makes a cup of coffee, chugs it, and he's out of there. Parks at Eddie's, walks to the door. Locked. He pounds on it a couple times and Eddie opens up, unshaven, not usual for him, lets him in.

"What the fuck time is it?" Tommy says.

"Eight."

"Jesus." Tommy shakes his head. "You got a pot of

coffee, I hope."

"Behind the bar. Take a seat. Want anything in it?"

"Jameson's."

Eddie nods, pours two cups, adds a splash to one, sets it in front of Tommy. "What's in it for me?"

"First, don't fuck me on this. I got partners."

Eddie's voice rises. "They know my name?"

"Not yet. But if I get fucked, they get fucked. They figure it out."

"So, The Manatee? You pulled it? I ain't touchin' that fuckhole, Tommy."

"You put me in it, Eddie. You're in."

"What? Some guy I put you with? Ain't shit to do with me. I get my intro fee, though."

Tommy saw that coming, hands over the cash, talks again. "Joey Lee starts going through how shit ties together, good luck. I say, we dump it all on this Von motherfucker. He got ties with Joey's guy who got a piece a that place, plus everyone who died with him."

"But that's just the group tried to stop the robbery."

"That's the group crossed Joey. We gotta hope that's all he cares about. And you're in that we, Eddie. Help me with this, I get you a piece of the pie. Just need you to spread the word."

"How big a piece?"

"Five grand."

"Make it seven, I put it out there."

"I gotta talk to my guys but yeah, we can do that."

"I get mine up front. From you. They don't meet me. You explain it."

"Jesus, Eddie. Don't ask for much, do ya?"

"That's the deal."

"I need an hour to get the money."

"I'll be here."

Tommy goes back to his room. Amanda's still there. She's supposed to be but he didn't lock her up or give any orders. "You waited for me?"

"Don't wanna be home when whatever happens to Von…"

"Who knows what or when. Got nothin' to do with me."

"But you're makin' sure he gets blamed."

"Makin' sure I don't. Truth gets out, I'm fine."

She has a cup in her hand. The look in her eyes says she added booze to the coffee. "You're all about the truth now, ain'tcha Tommy?"

"Right now I'm all about gettin' in and out of here fast." He walks to the closet, opens the door.

She follows. "You leavin', Tommy?"

"Comin' back. Wait there. Right there." He glares at her and she stops. He dials the safe combination, opens it, counts out seven large and puts it in a pocket, shuts and locks the safe. He closes the closet door, walks past her. "Enjoy yer coffee."

She drinks. He drives to Eddie's and pays him off, gets out of there and calls the crew, tells everyone it's another seventeen fifty each to get Joey off them. Three phone calls, three times he says "We all meet together," and gives the time and place. Two hours, in case they ain't got the money on 'em. But he ain't walkin' around with three guys owin' him money any longer than he has to.

Lunch at Becky's: they open early, good food, quiet neighborhood where no one will fuck with you. It's in Rockridge so parking sucks but he'll eat enough to need the walk after. He don't need the walk before eating but he gets one. He's there before the rest of the crew, orders a table for four and a Tsing Tao, looks at the model boats hanging from the ceiling, mirrors on the walls, Chinese paper lamps over every table. Always liked this place.

His beer arrives and he drinks. Before he's half done the table is full, everyone with a beer.

"You hadda bring in another guy," Karma says. "Couldn't do this ourselves."

"I know a guy I trust, can get word to Joey fast. We die if that don't happen."

"I wanna meet the guy."

Tommy drinks, shrugs. "He don't wanna meet you."

"How do we know there's this other guy?"

"Fuck you ya think I'm lyin'. You believe me, Juke?"

"Hell yeah."

"Dunbar?"

Dunbar rubs his hand down his face. "I guess."

"You guess?"

"I don't know you, Tommy. Ain't your friend like Juke here."

"You sayin' we pullin' somethin'?"

"Ain't sayin' shit. Only, like Karma says, why can't we meet the guy?"

Tommy glares at Dunbar, then Karma. "You two think the guy who's gonna save our asses don't exist. Well maybe he don't if I come to you assholes first. Then it's too late and no one can save us. That's what I'm thinkin' when he says he gets the money up front. So I get him the money. Now I'm out seven large. Five 'n' a quarter, really, cuz the rest is my share. If I coulda paid him just my share and left you on your own, sounds like I shoulda. But it don't work that way. We all die or we all get through this."

"So, uh," Karma says, "you think all this cuz yer like a scientist and shit and the goddamn facts, they got weighed. But you ain't got time to call us before you make the deal? You sure as hell call fast enough when you need the money. How the fuck we know where this money's goin'? Or gone?"

The waitress comes over with more beers. "Are you ready to order?"

Four menus lie on the table, never picked up.

"Give us a few minutes, honey," Tommy says. "I'll wave."

"Okay." She smiles and Tommy likes it. She's pretty for an older broad. Hell, she might be Tommy's age.

He turns away quick when she leaves, looks at Karma again. Talks soft. "You don't trust me?"

"You know there's ways of doin' things, right? This ain't the right way."

"Get this straight. This is my job. I planned it, I run it. You worked it, that's all. I don't talk to the hired help when it's time to make a decision."

"This decision's about my money."

"The whole job's about *our* money. Mine's already paid on this part."

"Only, ain't like you can show us a receipt."

Tommy whispers. "You killed God knows how many men or maybe we don't gotta do this. Seventeen fifty ain't much for your life."

"You don't like how I work so we all gotta pay extra? That what this is?"

"What this is is simple. You're good with a gun, I get it. You reach in your pocket and you pull something ain't money, you can shoot fast. Only, I can see both your hands. You can only see one a mine. The other's under the table, a pistol pointed at your dick. You should trust me, Karma. I'm a good guy."

Karma nods slow. "You get paid."

"Now."

Karma looks around the room. No one pays attention to their table. He reaches inside his coat. Tommy watches close. *Don't do nothin' stupid, I like this place.* Karma lays an envelope in front of Tommy.

Tommy glances at Dunbar. "Yours on top of his."

Dunbar keeps his mouth shut, puts his envelope where he's told. Juke drinks his beer slow, like it means more to him than anything else at the table. He sets his glass down, adds an envelope to the pile, and Tommy pockets them all.

"I know what order the stack's in. Anyone shorted me ain't gonna live. I'm checkin' the count before we leave." No one answers. Tommy drinks. "Y'all might wanna look at those menus. Food's good."

He counts the cash after they order; the money's good too. The food arrives and only Juke eats with chopsticks. Tommy usually does but this time he takes a fork; it's hard to eat with chopsticks when one hand holds a pistol.

Becky's serves good portions but these are guys who eat—no unfinished meals here. They all kick in on the check, with extra for a tip. The pile of cash is taken away. Tommy sits until everyone else stands. No way he walks in front of Karma. This didn't go good; might not be worth what he collected. He ain't givin' it back though.

Outside there's no parking lot, just nice shopping district/residential sidewalk. Lunchtime not near as crowded as dinner, most people still at work. They walk wide on the sidewalk, Dunbar and Karma in front, Tommy and Juke behind.

Tommy slows a second, puts a hand on Juke's good shoulder, talks soft. "I turn when I reach the street I parked. Stay with Karma."

Juke nods and they catch up to Dunbar and Karma, same distance behind as they'd been. No one's talking. Food was the only thing about this that wasn't business. And now maybe sides have been chosen. That's up to Karma. Tommy's worried what happens if he leaves things to Karma. He reaches his street and takes it. Juke follows Karma and Dunbar. Tommy trusts Juke but he looks back the whole walk to his car.

The money's settled; he should go back to Carla and work things out. Only he can't do anything that brings Karma to his wife, his kid. Right when everything's about to fall on Von. Lucky he has Amanda; she don't matter as much. He goes back to his room, hopes she's there. No one else knows he has this, the one place he's safe.

He parks, goes to his door, walks inside. She's not waiting for him this time. He didn't say she couldn't leave, didn't feel like she wanted to. Only now he wants her and she's gone. Tommy finds a glass, fills it with bourbon—and shakes, the shit already bursting from his ass. He runs like hell for the toilet but the shit fills his pants and runs down his leg. He makes it to the bathroom and it's good he's alone for the removal of gross clothes, the cleaning of filthy body parts. Weird, his gut hasn't bugged him in days. Now he feels it flipping and hopes the damage is done.

So Amanda's gone and he don't want her to be and it

ain't just because he was in the mood for a fuck. She's on his side. He needs to keep her with him; any breath outside this room could be as bad as betrayal. Better keep her mouth shut. If Joey found out who pulled the job, Tommy was dead. They'd all be dead.

He already has to deal with Karma. But he sits convulsively shitting when what he needs is to get Carla back. And first he has to get Amanda so she don't talk, then he has to kill Karma. If he can ever stop—his hands grip the seat and his body slams forward, his ass thrusts back, he's empty and in pieces and he can see the shit in front of him on the floor and on his clothes and feel it bursting behind him and he can't do a goddamned thing until it stops. He's pretty sure Karma don't know where he is unless he comes across Amanda. Tommy tries to remember who knows Amanda.

He's falling, reaches out to brace himself. Hits the floor hard, it ain't a dream. He wakes fast, opens his eyes slow. His whole body aches. Not like a beating, just sore. Except his hands, they hurt worse, caught him when he fell. Always a bad move unless you value your face. Nothing broke so he's okay with this much pain, opens his eyes. Everything's blurry. A minute and he recognizes the bathroom floor. It's sideways is all.

He sits up, blinks a few times. Shit on the floor off to one side, shitted-on clothes beside it. Done that cleanup before, don't even need normal strength. What he needs strength for is killing Karma. And he'll need a plan. Never saw a guy that good with a gun. Tommy stares at the wall, shuts his eyes. Keeps staring, sees nothing. That's all he can think of, too. The best way to kill

Karma: nothing.

Tommy calls Juke, explains the problem. Where the hell does Karma have the money and how the hell do they get it? Tommy goes through this conversation twice. Hitting Karma's fine but it sounds like a losing bet. And if you can't kill a man like that, how you gonna rip him off?

Gotta get him out of his room. They're all crooks, stealing should be easy. They gotta meet again, talk out the details. It could be done over the phone, but Tommy don't trust phones.

A table at Jacks or Better, the last place anyone's gonna bother you. One by one they get their drinks at the bar.

Tommy's on his second beer, Dunbar barely on his first.

"Got an idea," Tommy says as Juke sits with a beer and a scotch. "You two meet with Karma and I search his place."

"Whatta we tell Karma?" Dunbar asks.

"Don't say shit. You're just waitin' for me same as him. Say I made it sound important, that's all."

Juke looks up from his scotch. "Who calls the meet?"

"I got to," Tommy says. "He knows it's my job. You guys meet him here, I go to his place. Send me a text when he shows. Don't say nothin'. Just hit send."

"But we do this." Dunbar talks slow, thinking it through. "And he gets ripped off, he gonna come for all of us. We don't do this, it's just you and him."

Tommy nods. "Yeah. Only you don't side with me on this, you got other problems. You're with me and Juke, or you're against us."

CHAPTER FIFTEEN

He don't need to case Karma's place, he's a thief and he cases everywhere he goes. He didn't go into Karma's bedroom before and he figures that's where the money's stashed. Unless the guy keeps it on him. Crazy mother-fucker might.

Tommy's in his hotel room. No wife, no kid, no pit bull, not even a girlfriend. Alone with a bottle, not the first time. And he needs Karma dead and he wants the money. So he has to call Karma—tomorrow, he's getting drunk tonight—he has to put something out there that makes him show.

At least this place has ESPN. He watches football highlights, football previews, plus all the shit sports they're trying to convert him to. Watches all that sports garbage and only thing matters is what he comes up with by morning.

When he wakes he's hungover but it ain't bad, his brain's alive. He has a coffee, makes the call while pouring the next.

Karma picks up on the third ring. "You got somethin' for me?"

"Yeah. All four of us meet and talk like we shoulda last time. So we all walk."

"And we meet where and when you say."

"You got a suggestion? I don't give a fuck."

"What's your idea?" Karma asks.

"Same place. Two o'clock."

"It's what, ten? How about we make it eleven."

"You're kiddin' me," Tommy says. "I gotta call the other guys. Make it twelve."

Like the meet is the hit. Like Karma thinks moving things up three hours changes anything. Tommy calls Juke and Dunbar while he drinks his coffee, makes himself some eggs and takes a shower. He's ready to steal fifteen large.

At eleven he waits in a doorway across the street from Karma's. Juke's gonna text him when Karma gets to the meet but he can't wait that long; he wants to see the man leave. His car's around the corner behind Karma's building. Only way he gets noticed is if Karma looks right at him.

Eleven-thirty and Karma's out the front door and into the garage, drives out in a black Mercedes. Motherfucker don't do nothin' quiet.

He's gone five minutes when Tommy goes to the building's front door. All those buttons to push and wait for someone to buzz him in. Front door locked he looks around, sees no one, tries a credit card. Don't want an obvious break-in. Karma's gonna know when his money's gone though.

Tommy presses buzzers. He knows Karma ain't the type to talk to neighbors, presses thirty-nine, the highest number on the list. No way the guy's said a word to someone on a different floor. "Hey," he says into the box, "I'm in eleven, locked myself outta the building. Buzz me in?"

Not a lot of people home this time of day, he works his way down to twenty-seven and someone buzzes back, don't say a word. He walks down the hall to number eleven. It's locked, but that thing Karma said about anyone could pick it? He didn't lie, the thing's really fuckin' basic and Tommy's inside.

He heads for the bedroom and opens the door slow, steps in. Decent room with a decent-looking dresser across from the queen-size bed, a closet with sliding doors off to the side. Everything nice wood, stained the same shade of brown. Even the little bedside table but no lamp, like the table came with the room. Bare walls, no windows; the man sleeps here but it ain't like he does much else.

Maybe Karma checks the money soon as he gets home but Tommy got no reason to make it obvious. So he looks at the mattress careful before he flips it— nothing there—and puts it back same as it was. Empties dresser drawers the same. Goes through the closet, every inch of the room, hits the walls and floors for dead spots. No false bottoms nowhere, no nothin'. And Karma ain't the kind of guy to keep that kind of cash nowhere he can't reach.

Fuck, he lost track of time. Twelve-thirty and no word from Juke. He sends a text, gets one right back. *He ain't here yet.* And Tommy knows he should get the fuck out. He's in the living room only now he ain't so tidy, throws things and don't put them back, cuts into the couch's lining and turns it upside down, furniture's everywhere and the money ain't there and he's in the bathroom and the money ain't there and he knows

Karma got it on him and what's that motherfucker doing now? Tommy leaves the place a mess, swings the door hard behind him and bolts out of there to his car, drives away. He called the meet, he hit Karma's place, that much is obvious. Karma's after him and on the run at the same time. And Tommy ain't got a clue where the man is.

Tommy can't go nowhere he's known. The place he's staying is cool, no one knows but Amanda. Fuck, where's she? If Karma knows about her...He drives, calls her and puts it on speaker. It rolls to voicemail. "Call me. Now."

He gets off the main road soon as he can, pulls over outside some random house, calls and starts talking soon as Juke picks up. "Hey man, we gotta be in the wind, no telling what he got in mind. Me for sure, you maybe, maybe even Dunbar. No places he knows, but we can meet."

"Yeah, we're outta there. Want me to choose a place? You might have to wear grown-up clothes. You got a reason we need to meet?"

"Nah. Not yet. Gotta find my woman before he does."

"Carla?"

"Nah, other woman."

Fuck, though. The house. That's public information, Karma could go there easy. Tommy turns his car around and ends the call with Juke.

Carla's cell rolls straight to voicemail. "Don't go home. Not Malik either. I call when it's safe."

He picks up speed and drives to the house, parks right in front. He won't be here long; if he's seen, he's seen. He runs to the front door, unlocks it, and opens it slow. Rommel looks at him, follows Tommy as he grabs poop bags and treats. Tommy leashes Rommel and walks him to the car, opens the back door and pats the seat with one hand. Rommel leaps and lies down on the seat. Tommy gets in front and drives away.

Filled with the thought, *How do I kill Karma?* Get away from this house for starters, so he don't kill me. But there was also the thought he should circle back, get Karma from behind. Back of the head's only way he knows he can take him.

Gotta handle this quick. No matter what he says Carla won't stay out of the house long, and she brings Malik back with her. Where else they gonna stay, what else can he tell her? Kill Karma soon and let her know it's cool to go home, work his way back to her. That's what this whole job's about, getting back with Carla. God she's beautiful. Too bad she likes to stay sober.

He wishes he had a bottle with him now, feels the surge in his gut and hopes he can drive. He shakes, struggles to hold the wheel steady, explodes shit all down his pants and onto the car floor, pulls over. He's gonna kill that motherfucker Karma, that's all there is to it. This stress is gonna ruin his upholstery.

He pulls up Karma's number, calls.

"What?"

"You don't show up at my fuckin' meet. We gotta talk."

"Why?"

"Not on the phone. That's why we meet."

"You want this too much."

"Choose the place, asshole. Choose the time. Shoot me in the back of the fuckin' head. We talk to each other or we all get killed."

Karma's quiet half a minute. "What's Joey know?"

"Not over the phone. Where? When?"

"The place you stay."

"My house? When?"

"Nah," Karma says, "where you are now."

"That's over. I'm back at the house. You know it."

"With the woman and kid?"

"They're gone," Tommy says. "When?"

"You there now?"

"What the fuck you care? When?"

"Call you back." Karma ends the call.

Tommy gets out of the car, walks passenger side and shakes his pants as clean as he can. Hose himself down and the car if he could. Karma goes away, all this stress does too. He gets back in and heads back toward the house, music loud and windows down so he can breathe easy, Rommel behind him. Someone might die tonight; it won't be that dog.

Tommy parks in the driveway but watches the house from almost a block away, behind a stranger's car across the street. An hour later Karma's car rolls past the house. A few minutes after that Karma enters the driveway on foot.

Rommel behind him, Tommy steps fast toward the house.

Karma approaches the house slow, runs to the car in the driveway and squats beside it, moves forward in a crouch. He reaches the hood and runs to the front door. It's unlocked. He enters.

Tommy runs to the car, Rommel jogging behind him. They run nowhere near as fast as Karma, Tommy's pants already crusty. They reach the front door and Tommy stands, wishes some of the dried shit would drop to the porch.

The door shut in front of him, Tommy takes a deep breath and pushes it open. Along the wall, Rommel to his left, he steps slow to the edge of the living room.

Karma turns and smiles, pistol in his right hand alongside his thigh.

Tommy takes a step away from the wall, his pistol positioned the same as Karma's but Karma's pistol rises fast, aims at Tommy's head, only there's a growl and Karma looks down.

Rommel's right in front of him, jaws wide. He stares at Karma's crotch.

Tommy shakes his head, eyes on Karma. "I say the word, he tears it off. I came to talk."

Karma lowers his pistol, nods. "We talk."

"Put your pistol on the floor. You know the deal."

"What about your gun?" Karma says. "How we gonna work the rest of this deal?"

"We gonna work it so Rommel here don't eat your dick. Put it on the floor."

"My dick?" Karma says, but he opens his hand and squats with the trigger guard dangling from his index finger, the gun otherwise untouched as he lays it on the floor. "And you ain't gonna kill me."

"We got enough bodies on this." Tommy gestures with his pistol. "Get up."

Karma rises slow, a glance down at the weapon that's his best chance to stay alive.

"Kick it over there."

Tommy points with his empty hand and Karma kicks hard. The pistol tumbles awkwardly along the thin carpet, stops eight feet away.

Tommy shrugs. "Good enough. We're goin' out. You first." He waves forward and Karma walks, Rommel following. Tommy scoops Karma's pistol into a coat pocket and exits last, shuts the front door behind him.

"My car," Tommy says. "You ride shotgun. Don't wanna kill you, Joey comes at us we might need you. But don't fuck with me. Ain't no one lives forever."

Rommel watches Karma like a meal that's almost ready. Tommy drives.

Karma crinkles his nose. "Christ, you smell like shit again. What the fuck is wrong with you? Dyin' of somethin' or somethin'?"

"Been sick. Go to the doc when I get a chance."

"So, since that ain't gonna happen while we're in the middle of this what ya might call a situation here, I can roll down my window, right? Cuz I'm fuckin' gaggin'."

"Mine's down," Tommy says. "That's enough."

"Ya wanna tell me why not?"

"I don't trust you. Whatever you want, I don't."

"Truth is," Karma says, "your window down on the open road, I'm gettin' cold all a sudden. How about we roll all the windows up?"

"Now you're bein' funny? What the fuck is wrong with you? Joey Lee might want us dead." They hit open highway and Tommy accelerates.

"Can't do nothin' 'bout what the man wants. I'm just passin' time best I can. That's all I did when I was inside, all I do now I'm out. You drink and fuck, right? That's what I do, drink with people and fuck with people."

"Thing is," Tommy says, "we gotta lay low right now. Word gets out this guy Von's behind The Manatee job, we're in the clear. Joey knows Von. He's gonna see this as betrayal. Von denies it, he just might die slower. We gotta give it time, for word to get to Joey and for him to believe it."

"Thing you gotta remember," Karma says, the wind blowing in Tommy's window but getting nowhere near Karma, "there's a money end to this deal and Joey Lee's a boss and ain't a boss lived don't care about the money. He guts Von's place and The Manatee money ain't there, he's gonna keep lookin'."

"Hits that place he's gonna find money. Ain't like it's tagged where it come from. Von does alright, money's somewhere. Only way he lasts long enough to hurt us is someone believes him. Ain't gonna happen so long's Joey got him, and it ain't comin' up before. And after? He can't convince no one of nothin'."

"You know a lotta smart guys, Tommy? You think they always believe what they hear first? A man like Joey Lee, finds out he killed the wrong guy? He goes back, kills the right guy. He ain't gotta worry 'bout lookin' bad in the fuckin' newspapers or on the fuckin' internet or whatever fuckin' pack a lies where people get their news these days. You been doin' this how long and you think that's how it's done down here? You know what word on the street is like; always changin', always someone doin' shit cuz they believe it. You ain't totally stupid, you say you want me with you in case Joey Lee. And yeah, Joey come at us, I can hold off some guys, but he wants us dead? We just passin' time."

Tommy shakes his head like that might get rid of the headache Karma's giving him. "We gonna do it my way." His eyes on the road. "Or I give your balls to Rommel here and maybe you live, maybe you don't. I give it some time and see before I shoot you in the head."

"Y'know, Tommy?" Karma puts an arm around him; Rommel growls. "There's a lotta ways I could die. You killin' me ain't one of 'em. My name rings out, yours don't. You don't know what's real in this world, I ain't surprised. What's real is, you never gonna kill me. You ain't a killer. Might shoot some punk, won't do shit to a guy like me. Joey Lee? Yeah, he got guys, that shit makes sense. You shoot me, you wind up dead. Ain't no other result. You seen what happens when people shoot at me? I got the power, motherfucker."

"Rommel don't give a fuck 'bout your power."

"You're a dead asshole soon enough, Tommy. But it won't be me, and I'm with you past when Joey Lee takes the bait. We gonna keep this money."

"You think Joey won't figure it out."

Karma shrugs. "Someone try to put me somewhere, I put him there first. How I don't get shot, you know. Things I believe in protect me."

"Sounds like some kinda hippie bullshit."

"I don't get shot and I don't get played."

"You done time."

"That's before," Karma says. "Inside's a place a man learns. Sure, what a lotta guys learn's just how to do their jobs better. And a lotta guys find Jesus. Or somethin'. What I find, you know, maybe it don't work for everybody, a belief is a thing works for the guy believes it. I just tell you, I'm good at what I believe. If it ever wasn't gonna work, I'd be dead a few times now."

"That don't make no sense."

"I ain't about makin' sense. I'm playin' games and I'm playin' people and I'm playin' the world. Try to play me, you gonna lose. But I like the move you made with that dog. Smart play, why I wanna stick with you."

"Hah. Rommel eats your dick you gonna want me to shoot you in the head."

"Sometimes you think good, Tommy, but you don't *know*. I know. Still wanna work with a smart player."

"You believe in magic like a fuckin' idiot. You know Joey Lee can kill us."

"Joey got a power too. You think it's just he's a boss and he got all these guys work for him. Nah, what Joey got like what I got, I can feel it. That shit ever goes down, he got power *and* numbers. I just got power."

Tommy smirks. "Bull. Shit. But we're on the same side, we ain't gotta agree about why."

"So, where we goin', partner?"

"You stay with me and Rommel. Trust is great. Let you know when we have it."

Tommy pulls up to a motel. He and Karma go in and register, one room. Two beds but it's Oakland, the guy at the counter don't give a fuck, just wants a credit card.

Tommy elbows Karma.

"Ain't got one."

"You serious?"

"Anyone wanna find me, let 'em look."

"Jesus."

Tommy uses a card, gets a key, and they get back in the car with Rommel, drive around the corner and park near their room. It's a no pets policy but no one sees them and if they did, Tommy and Karma with a pit bull don't look like guys anyone says shit to.

The door shut behind them, Tommy waves his pistol. "The bathroom."

"You serious? You ain't this stupid."

Pistol pointed at his head, Karma walks into the bathroom.

Tommy's a few feet behind him. "Put the stopper in the tub and run the cold water. An inch high."

It gets to about half that. "Turn it off." Karma does. "Rommel."

The dog looks at him. Tommy points to the tub. "In, boy."

Rommel puts his forepaws on the bathtub ledge, looks at the water below and leaps in. Water splashes but not out of the tub. Rommel drinks.

"You are one weird motherfucker, Tommy."

CHAPTER SIXTEEN

Rommel lies between the beds. Tommy sits on the edge of one, Karma on the other. A fifth of bourbon, no glasses, Tommy drinks from the bottle then passes it to Karma. No one's said a word since the last time Karma bitched about Tommy smelling like shit. The news is on TV but a hit Joey Lee calls will be just another quiet Oakland murder.

Without talk, the bottle's going fast. It's a fifth, so there's still plenty left and the booze is kicking in.

"News don't say shit," Tommy says.

"We need word on the street."

"Then we gotta be on the street. Easy targets."

"Stayin' here's hidin'." Karma straightens from his slouch. "We oughta be on the street."

"Too soon. Juke knows without me sayin', Dunbar better know too. Juke'll tell me anything goes wild. Stays quiet a couple days, someone gotta talk to Carelli."

"That little fuck?"

"He knows everything, I don't care how he gets it. I'll even talk to him on this."

"Even?"

"Had a thing went kinda sour, got straightened. You tell me: you got someone else might know what Joey's up to?"

Karma nods. "The shit with Von, guys might know."

"A guy knows more than Carelli, drop his name. Or two days from now, I see that motherfucker myself."

Two days is a long time in a cheap motel room, longer with two men who don't trust each other and a pit bull who needs periodic long walks. Tommy stinks. So the walks are a relief for everyone, but Tommy's ready to shoot Karma every step of the way.

They don't run at all, which is what Rommel really wants, so they walk extra miles like that's enough. Hours outside and they need it, with a stop on the way for a fresh bottle, Rommel tethered outside ready to kill anyone who might try to steal him. Tommy bought a bag of dog food the first day so they're good on that.

Back in the little room, Tommy checks there's still water in the tub then he and Karma are back at their spots on the beds, trading swigs.

"Ain't it the time," Karma says, "you was gonna meet with that little wop?"

"Wop? Ain't you Italian?"

"A wop knows a wop."

"So the thing, ya wop fuck, I ain't leavin' you to meet Carelli and he don't like crowds. Waitin' for a call from Juke. Then we know what's goin' down. Before it's on the street."

"So he's meeting Carelli?"

"Should be done soon."

They drink while they wait. A few slugs each but they're going fast.

An hour and Tommy's phone rings. He pulls his pistol

and points it at Karma then picks up. "Yeah?"

"We're fucked," Juke says. "Get out."

Tommy ends the call, takes the bottle from Karma and drinks, pushes the lid back on, nods at Karma to stand and leashes Rommel. "To the car. Fast."

In the car, same positions as before, Tommy turns to Karma. "Joey's after us. I'm gettin' my wife and kid. After that, where you wanna be dropped?"

"We gettin' the woman who kicked you out? While I'm here?"

"You wanna die now?"

"Just sayin', this how you convincin' her back?"

Tommy keeps driving. "That's where we're goin'." He brakes at the red light.

Karma swings his left arm hard across Tommy's neck. Tommy's gasping for breath as Karma climbs over him, Rommel snarling and craning but unable to reach as Karma hurls himself out the open window of the slow rolling car. Tommy straightens the wheel with one hand and grabs his pistol with the other but Karma's rolled and jumped up on the pavement and swerves to the right. Tommy fires once on a prayer, hits nothing, tries again, still no luck. He straightens the car only now Karma's gone. He returns the gun to its holster.

We're all dead, Tommy thinks, and drives toward home. But he can't go there. There's either someone waiting now and he'll get popped if he shows up, or he gets there before them and they go in behind him. He goes to the house, he might be bringing death to everyone in it.

He turns the car around and calls Juke. It rings a few times, rolls to voicemail. "Call me back."

He drives back toward his usual stretch of town. His regular spots won't be safe, but where else can he go?

Not Chinatown: that's Joey's base.

He can't just drive not knowing where but fifteen minutes and Juke ain't called back. He calls Eddie.

Third ring, Eddie picks up. "Yeah?" There's music and voices in the background.

"It's Tommy. We gotta talk. You workin'?"

"Always. Come over."

"What happened with that thing you did for me?"

"It got done. I'm busy. You wanna talk, c'mere."

"Nah. Berkeley. When can you be there?"

"Berkeley? I hate fuckin' Berkeley. Call me tomorrow." Eddie ends the call.

Fuck his usual haunts, Tommy's driving to Berkeley. Keene's home turf, not Joey Lee's. Those two are at war and this shouldn't be worth Joey's time. Closest he can come to safe. Might as well get a bottle and sleep tonight.

Tommy wakes fully dressed on a made bed, half a fifth of bourbon on the bedside table. He takes a shot from the bottle—good stuff—and caps it. There's a checkout at eleven notice next to the bottle with the name of the motel and a University Avenue address. He looks at his phone: 10:50. Fuck.

He stands, the smell of shit all around him, feels it in his clinging pants but there's no time for a shower. He takes a step away from the bed and his foot comes down on a beer bottle. Wobbling, he holds his arms out for balance, stays on his feet. Kicks the bottle aside, don't recognize the label that rolls away, steps back to the bed and retrieves the bourbon. He looks at the floor as he works his way to the door, sees four more empties but no way he bends over to ID 'em, his gut hurts something awful. Whatever that brand is, it worked. He remembers the liquor store clerk recommended it—the selection was huge—and he don't remember much since.

He walks outside and dammit he's on the second floor. Rommel stands steady beside him, the leash trailing. Tommy shudders and grabs the rail. The walkway looks over the parking lot. He shakes and he's shitting again. Most of the spasm is in his gut, not much comes out his ass. Good thing, he can barely stand the smell of himself already. The spasm stops and he moves along the rail hand over hand, reaches the stairs and turns sideways, goes down the same way.

In the car he rolls the windows down and stuffs the bourbon under the passenger seat before he hits the gas. Now he needs to meet Eddie but he can't do it smelling like this.

There has to be somewhere to buy clothes downtown. Not much traffic but he drives slow, only a couple blocks and he sees a thrift store but nowhere to park. He makes a right at the next corner and circles around, parks in a restaurant loading zone, leaves Rommel in the car.

Inside, the thrift store ain't even musty with old clothes. He brings his own stench. He grabs one T-shirt, a half dozen pairs of pants close to his size and a couple pairs of sweatpants and walks to the register. The cashier gets more than a whiff of him and her eyes go wide. "Jesus, Mister, you okay?"

A lot of homeless live down this way so he knows he looks bad. "Ring me up, honey." He peels a few twenties from his wallet and knows he don't look homeless and maybe that's worse to this woman. Fuck it, he'll be fine if Joey Lee don't kill him.

He goes back to the car, drops his bag of clothes on

the passenger seat, ignores the ticket on his windshield and gets out his phone. He needs a bathroom to clean up and no restaurant's gonna let him in. He looks up the nearest library. Another ten minutes driving and he parks five blocks from it, grabs the t-shirt and one pair of pants from his bag and walks, Rommel asleep on the back seat. No one's stealing that car.

There's a group of homeless guys outside a library door that says No Entrance. He's sure they know where the men's room is but he ain't talking to these pathetic fucks. He walks in the front door. A security guy's there and the guy glances at him but don't say a word, more concerned with people going out.

Sign next to an elevator says the men's room is on two. He goes up, finds his way. Urinals, a sink, and an empty stall. He soaks the t-shirt and goes into the stall, drops the toilet seat and takes off his shoes and socks, sets them on it. Gross place to stand barefoot but inside his pants is worse. He pushes with one hand and steps out when they hit the floor.

The other hand holds the clean pants and wet t-shirt. He sets the pants on top of the toilet and wipes down his ass and legs until they're as clean as he can get them. Now it's the shirt that's disgusting. He holds out his arm and drops it on the floor.

Puts on the new pants. A little loose. Takes his belt off the shit-stained pants and puts it on the new ones, puts on his socks and shoes, leaves the shitty shirt and pants on the floor and walks out of the stall.

Back on the sidewalk he stares down the homeless ass-holes and calls Eddie.

"What the fuck?" Eddie says. "This ain't morning."

"Close as I could do. Gotta see you, Eddie."

"Not much time now. I gotta work tonight. Triple Rock, twelve-thirty?"

"Yeah, sure. I'll be at the bar."

"No shit." Eddie ends the call.

Tommy don't know many details in Berkeley but he knows Triple Rock. Walking distance from where he is now. And he has time to walk there, gets back in his car instead.

He circles to Berkeley Way, pulls into a pay lot, puts a card in the machine. Two hours. Triple Rock's a half block from here.

It's early and there's a decent lunch crowd at the tables but the bar's near empty. Place is bigger than he remembers; they added another room? Don't matter to him, he orders a house IPA for breakfast.

He's on his second when Eddie walks in.

"We get a table," Eddie says and they go to the back of the room, where it's empty.

Eddie says, "Whaddaya want?"

"I gotta know." Tommy talks soft but a waiter's right there.

"There's no table service here until after five but you can order at the bar." He holds out two menus.

"We're good," Eddie says.

Something about his voice: the waiter takes a step back. "Just wave if you need anything." He takes another backward step and turns away.

"Gotta know what?" Eddie says.

"Word on the street. About Von. And me and my guys."

"Von ain't been seen in a couple days. Pretty sure he

213

had visitors. You, I ain't heard shit about."

"So it might be safe."

"Might's a big fuckin' word, Tommy. You want information, I work in a bar. Talk to the man who knows everything. 'Course, that puts you on the street."

"Unless you gimme his number."

"You think guys who get that number can give it out? Jesus, Tommy, you need a fuckin' cuppa coffee. Maybe try Starbucks, I hear they're good."

Early afternoon, Carelli's at his table. His usual coffee and newspaper in front of him, he takes a bite from a hot dog they definitely don't sell at Starbucks, gestures for Tommy to sit. He chews and swallows. "What now?" He drinks coffee.

Tommy sits. "Gotta know if there's anything on the street about me."

"You bring a envelope?"

"Yeah."

"Go to the head, fill it with half a g."

"How much extra to get updates on Juke and Karma?"

"I gotta call you? Another g."

"You want I should write down my number?"

Carelli shakes his head. "Just fuckin' tell me."

Tommy says it.

"Put the rest in the same envelope, I call you when things change."

Tommy stands.

"Code's five-six-seven-eight-nine."

Tommy walks inside, presses the code at the men's room door, enters. Someone's in the stall. He faces a wall, pulls out his envelope, puts fifteen hundreds inside and goes back to Carelli's table, sets the envelope on the newspaper.

Carelli peeks, counts the bills and pockets the envelope. Talks soft. "It's The Manatee. Von's guys died outside. No one buys they pulled it. Most guys don't care. Joey Lee does. Don't know what his boys did with Von, but they looked at his wife too. So, you and her's a known thing."

"And?"

"They know your crew. Whacked one of 'em. Dunbar."

"Shit. Joey thinks we pulled the job?"

"That man don't get played. By now he got Dunbar's share. You best run."

Cesar Chavez Park is at the Marina and part of it's an off-leash dog park that goes right up to the water. There's parking in a lot shared with boats and he pulls in, gets out with Rommel, and makes a call. She don't pick up.

"Hey Carla. We gotta get outta here. Meet me in Berkeley, we get two rooms at the Doubletree. I can explain. Not on the phone. I got money."

He takes Rommel into the park, a little ways before the off-leash area but he lets the dog go. Rommel heels. Tommy hopes she says yes to the Doubletree. That joint got rooms they letcha bring a dog. Malik can sleep in the room with the dog. Tommy wants Carla.

A step inside the off-leash area Tommy says "Go," and Rommel runs. Tommy jogs twenty yards for the stretch, stops to watch Rommel run off with a Rottweiler. The two dogs run together fifty yards then the Rott turns back and Rommel turns with him. They run toward a smiling woman twenty yards away.

Tommy'd barely noticed her but the dogs run fast and he takes a better look. She's about forty, fit and round, in jeans and a blue T-shirt that hangs. He watches Rommel run toward her with the Rott. He walks behind the dogs.

The dogs run past the woman and turn up a trail that leads farther from the entrance, toward the water. Tommy walks faster as the woman turns to join the dogs. He raises his voice. "Your Rott?"

"Yes," she says, turns to the dogs ahead and walks.

Tommy keeps walking fast but he ain't gaining much. If she don't want to be hit on that's okay with him. She's pretty enough but he don't expect nothing. He just likes dogs. He's waiting for Carla to call back and if there's something nice to look at he's good with that. And following this woman ain't a bad view.

When he gets outta here he gotta get out fast, and a long way. Sooner he leaves the better but he's gotta take Carla with him. And Malik. Dunbar's already dead and he hopes Juke makes it out but it ain't the worst thing if Karma dies alone.

The hill ain't steep and she walks steady but Tommy's legs loosen and he picks up speed, gets close behind her just as the dogs come into view. "What's the Rott's name?"

"Artemis." Her eyes stay on the dogs.

"Like in Wild Wild West?"

She looks at him at last, eyebrows raised. "Artemis was the Greek goddess of the hunt."

216

Tommy nods. He don't want a war here. "Mine's Rommel."

"Rommel? Like the Nazi?"

"The good Nazi. He was in a plot to kill Hitler."

They keep walking. The dogs have run off into the brush, can't be seen from the trail.

Tommy and the woman reach the top of the hill. She stops and Tommy stops with her. They can hear the dogs playing in the weeds.

"She always needs extra brushing after we come here." A sudden look at Tommy. "Your dog's fixed, right?"

"Hell yeah."

"And you're not a Nazi."

"I'm married, lady. And my wife's black. Whadda you think?"

She shakes her head. "Sorry. Some men talk so much bullshit. Then you defend a Nazi."

"Rommel was a soldier who loved his country. He didn't know what Hitler was doing. He was a military tactician."

"And that's a good thing."

Tommy lets out a deep breath. "When you're at war it is." He grumbles it, looks at his phone. Sees right away there's no calls, not even a text. He keeps looking, presses a button. Looks up. "I gotta go. Have a good hunt. Rommel! Come!"

Rommel runs out of the brush to him, the Rott trailing. Tommy and Rommel walk away.

Tommy calls the Doubletree, books a dog-friendly double with an adjoining single, tonight only. Not much of a risk. She don't meet him, he's fucked anyway. He's done everything she wants and now they have to leave together. A good night in a nice hotel near the freeway, they're over the bridge and into the city early morning then up the coast to somewhere no one'll ever find 'em.

Three-thirty now, the room ain't ready and Tommy ain't had lunch. He drives up University a mile or two, sees a burrito joint and parks at the first space he sees. He gets a carne asada with extra hot sauce, unwraps the foil enough to take a bite before he's back outside. Not great but it's a burrito and he's starved. He takes a couple more bites before he reaches the car and drives up to the pet supply place he saw on the way to the Marina, buys a roll of shit bags and bowls for food and water. Keeps heading toward downtown, swings a U when he sees that good liquor store, buys a six-pack of the same beer and another fifth just in case.

Takes a slug from his open fifth as he drives, another as he pulls into the Doubletree lot and parks. He closes the bourbon, opens a beer and the back door driver's side, fills the dog food bowl and sets it on the pavement beside his car.

"Down."

Rommel lands beside his food and eats. He's done with it long before Tommy finishes his burrito and beer. Their room won't be ready for a while. Tommy returns the food bowl to the car, throws on his jacket, grabs Rommel's leash, puts the shit bags in one side pocket and his open beer in the other. He locks the car and they walk back to the dog park. Ain't far and Rommel can get water there.

Five-thirty when they get back, still no word from Carla.

Tommy puts Rommel in the car long enough to check in.

"Shakowski," he says at the desk. "My rooms ready?"

The woman checks, confirms his credit card. "A double and single, pet friendly." She hands him a key for each. "Will you need additional keys?"

"When the wife and kid get here. Just me and the dog for now."

He gets his booze and dog bowls in the room first, goes back to the car and gets Rommel and his food, heads straight to the shitter as soon as they're inside. Not that crazy burst like he's sick, just a spicy burrito and how he washed it down. This is kind of comfortable, only half-bursting out of him. He hears his phone ring where he left it by the bed. No way he gets up in the middle of this. She never leaves a message but it better be her.

After a few minutes he finishes, cleans himself good. It ain't enough. He takes off his clothes, gets in the shower. Ten minutes later he's clean and dry. He drops the towel on the bathroom floor and walks to the bed, checks the missed call on his phone, calls her back.

She picks up. "You took Rommel?"

God she sounds hot when she's pissed. But—"You went to the house?"

"Of course we're at the house, Tommy. Where else we gonna be?"

"It ain't safe there."

"Ain't been safe the whole time we been here. And you're at the Doubletree? Registered as who?"

"Tommy Shakowski."

"Yeah, you're cautious as all hell. See you soon."

The call ends. He takes a drink straight from the bottle, carries it with him to the bathroom and puts his clothes back on. He takes another drink as he steps into the bedroom.

Rommel looks at him intently from where he lies at the foot of the bed.

"It's good, boy. We're all gonna be a family again."

Carla knocks. "Are you dressed?"

"You care? Come in."

"You invited me and Malik, remember?"

"I'm dressed. Come in."

The door handle drops and opens slow, like she don't believe him. Then her head's in the gap alongside the door and she pushes it open the rest of the way.

He sits on the bed, on the edge nearest the door, fully dressed but barefoot. He'd never lied as much as she thought.

She walks in and the door shuts behind her. Rommel walks to her and sits at her feet, his head up, watching.

"Hey," he says, "where's Malik?"

"Not here, Tommy. He's not coming."

"Why not? Where is he?"

"I said I'd come. I'm here."

"But you said that thing about Malik. Before you came in."

"I was trying to give you a chance. To be sober when I got here." She points at the bedside table. "Two open bottles. I know what you say you want. You don't want *me*."

"That ain't true."

"Go fuck a stranger, Tommy. That's what you want. Give me the leash."

"I don't wanna fuck just anyone."

"Give me the leash. We're done. And he's Malik's dog."

Tommy's head drops. His voice with it. "At least take some money."

"I don't want your fucking money. If you're in danger, deal with it. Keep it away from my family."

She clips the leash to Rommel's collar and steps toward the door.

Tommy stands, reaches for her.

Rommel turns at Tommy and growls, teeth bared. Tommy sits and Rommel walks out the door with Carla.

He's fucked now no matter what. His wife and son gone. Juke and Karma could get killed and he don't care about Karma except it means what Carelli said is true. Like there's a chance Carelli is wrong on this. On anything.

He drinks. All he can do is leave. He has money but he's gonna drink now. Carla's gone, the bourbon's what he has. He's here for the night or he dies on the road. Sets an alarm on his phone and scrolls through his contacts. No reason to leave alone if he don't have to. He calls Amanda. She picks up.

"You okay?"

"Fuck you, Tommy. Von—"

"You don't know and I don't know. We're on the phone, don't be stupid. You okay?"

"Fuck."

"I'm at the Doubletree, Berkeley Marina. Blowin' town tomorrow. Show up. There's plenty to drink and plenty more for the road."

"You want me there."

"Yeah."

"You killed my husband."

"He tried to kill me. I didn't do shit. We're on the

phone, shut up."

"That your romantic talk?" She's crying. "Someone else killed him, shut up?"

His phone rings. The other line's Carelli. "Hang on."

"Yeah."

He puts her on hold, picks up. "Yeah?"

"Juke's in a accident on the 80. Ain't gonna make it."

"Fuck. Karma?"

"No word yet."

Tommy switches back to Amanda. Dead line. He calls her back, it rolls to voicemail. "Come tonight," he says. "Or I'm gone." But he knows she ain't comin' and he's gone no matter what.

Alarm goes off at eight. He feels dead, shuts it off. Knows he should be in the car. Only one gun but plenty of money. What he needs now is coffee and a place to drop some cash on weapons.

He puts water and a bag of coffee in the coffee maker across the room. He's in the shower by the time it drips, out by the time it's ready. He fills the tiny cup and hopes it's cool enough to drink by the time he's dressed.

Hungover but he dresses fast, wishes he brought a change of socks. He'll buy some clothes when he gets wherever he's going. For now he takes a sip of hot coffee, slips into his shoes, and inventories the booze. No beers left, but most of the new fifth. Good, he'll need it.

He finishes the coffee, bags the bourbon, leaves the dog bowls and food behind and walks out the door. Another coffee for the road would be good but there's nothing between here and the freeway. He's gonna go north is all he knows for sure. Walks out of the hotel and into the parking lot. Everything about this is fucked. Except the money, he still has the money.

He opens the driver's side door, gets in, and sets his bag of bourbon on the passenger seat. Might need some before he gets anywhere. His keys in the ignition, he senses someone in back. He could fight but what difference does it make? He sits still, waits for what he deserves, don't wait long. A shot to the back of his head. He crumples and the guy's out of the car, leaves his door open then gets in the passenger seat.

Tommy's dying and this asshole's going through his pockets for the money. He's already lost Carla, Juke, Amanda, Malik, even Rommel. Every reason to stay alive. And they were all right to leave him.

If he's lucky his body gets dumped somewhere and no one finds him.

The cash woulda paid for a nice funeral.

ACKNOWLEDGMENTS

Thanks to Sean Craven and Tammy Chalala for helping to edit this book I otherwise wrote alone.

ROB PIERCE wrote the novels *Uncle Dust* and *With the Right Enemies*, the novella *Vern in the Heat*, and the short story collection *The Things I Love Will Kill Me Yet*. Rob has also edited dozens of novels freelance and for All Due Respect, and has had stories published in numerous ugly magazines. He lives and will probably die in Oakland, California.

On the following pages are a few
more great titles from the
Down & Out Books publishing family.

For a complete list of books and to
sign up for our newsletter,
go to DownAndOutBooks.com.

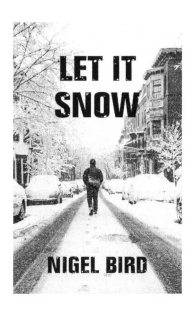

Let It Snow
Nigel Bird

Down & Out Books
November 2019
978-1-64396-047-0

A police officer is murdered while talking down a suicidal teenager. A rhino is killed at the zoo and has its horn removed. The biggest store in the city is robbed by a mannequin and record snowfall has created chaos within the police department.

As detectives seek the perpetrators of these crimes, they reflect upon their lives. Each of them needs to make changes. Not all of them know where to begin.

It's going to be one hell of a Christmas.

The Big Crescendo
Jonathan Brown

Down & Out Books
November 2019
978-1-64396-048-7

Lou Crasher is a wise cracking, drummer turned P.I. Drop dead gorgeous vocalist Angela, gets her musical instruments stolen. Lou vows to find them. He manages to uncover a gear-theft ring, a deadly drug cartel and accepts a risky offer from a big time music producer.

Lou's got one shot to get the gear, the girl and live to drum another day.

The Hurt Business
Stories by Mike Miner

All Due Respect, an imprint of
Down & Out Books
978-1-948235-75-4

"We are such fragile creatures."

The men, women and children in these stories will all be
pushed to the breaking point, some beyond. Heroes, villains
and victims. The lives Miner examines are haunted by pain
and violence. They are all trying to find redemption. A few
will succeed, but at a terrible price. All of them will face the
consequences of their bad decisions as pipers are paid and
chickens come home to roost. The lessons in these pages are
learned the very hard way. Throughout, Miner captures the
savage beauty of these dark tales with spare poetic prose.

40 Nickels
A Carnegie Fitch Mystery Fiasco
R. Daniel Lester

Shotgun Honey, an imprint of
Down & Out Books
978-1-948235-16-7

Carnegie Fitch can be called a lot of things. Ambitious is not one of them.

Months after escaping death in the circus ring at the hands of the Dead Clowns and the feet of a stampeding elephant, he is no longer a half-assed private eye with an office and no license, but instead a half-assed tow truck driver without either. Still, he daydreams about landing that BIG CASE.

Well, careful what you wish for, Fitch.

Made in the
USA
Middletown, DE

76379111R00146